CAROLINA DAWN

Guy L. Pace

Copyright © 2018 Guy L. Pace

Cover Design by Scott Deyett

Edited by J. C. Wing Family Editors

Scripture taken from the Holy Bible, NEW INTERNATIONAL VERSION®, NIV® Copyright © 1973, 1978, 1984, 2011 by Biblica, Inc.® Used by permission. All rights reserved worldwide.
NEW INTERNATIONAL VERSION® and NIV® are registered trademarks of Biblica, Inc. Use of either trademark for the offering of goods or services requires the prior written consent of Biblica US, Inc. For more information, please visit the following website: http://www.biblica.com/en-us/the-niv-bible/previous-editions/

This is a work of fiction. Names, characters, places, brands, media, and incidents are either the product of the author's imagination or are used fictitiously. Any resemblance to similarly named places or to persons living or deceased is unintentional.

ISBN-13: 978-0-9978669-4-0

Library of Congress Control Number: 2018900107

I want to thank my wife, Connie Pace, and J. C. Wing Family Editors for their reads and edits, and Scott Deyett for the fantastic cover. Of course, all the glory goes to God.

To my grandchildren.

ONE

Life

The power went out. Again. Silence. Dark.

Amy Grossman dropped her gear bag on the bed and fumbled on the dresser for a candle and some matches. *I know better than this. Be prepared,* she chastised herself as she lit a candle. The power went out almost every day lately.

She trudged down the stairs, careful not to drip wax from the candle. She and Paul Shannon spent their free time after the Washington, D.C. mission trip helping their parents scavenge materials to maintain and repair their homes, add more solar panels to their arrays, and connect batteries for power storage. She made her way to the utility room by the light of the candle, then opened the door to the garage.

Before The Troubles, most of their power came from hydroelectric and nuclear generating plants in North Carolina. Now, some people dedicated to keeping those systems working trade with the community for services, food, and other goods. Coal, oil, and gas fueled sources for power were long disabled or abandoned.

The main problem, she thought as she opened the electrical panel and turned off the main switch and pulled the lock bar over, was the power lines and substations. She flipped the switch that put the solar powered storage batteries on line. The lights came back on. The dams and the nuke plants worked fine. The lines that brought the power, though, often failed due to weather or age. That grid went through two winters of North Carolina weather and hurricane seasons with minimal maintenance.

She went back into the house and got her gear bag from her bedroom. Her schedule included some trading at the open market, a meeting of the perimeter watch, then she and Paul would work on their gardens together. Gardening became the only quality time they got to spend together. Dates were rare. She thought back on her demands of Paul from more than a year ago as she left the house. She had no idea how things would change and how the future would be shaped.

Amy stood perimeter watches four days a week in addition to helping with community child care. Paul, when not on foraging trips, worked with the community defense team and helped manage the perimeter watches.

School was no longer a formal system. Children went to school every day except Sunday. The older children helped feed and care for the younger children. A few teachers provided texts, lessons, and guidance to help keep everyone busy and learning every day.

Amy's and Paul's parents worked with the leadership of the community to help organize maintenance and repair of buildings the community used, and helped new arrivals and families find and set up suitable houses in the community. One of those new arrivals came in last fall. Lucy. Amy's gut clenched when she thought of her.

Lucy came from the Boone area. Paul ran across her during a foraging trip and brought her back to the community. She had dark eyes, straight raven hair, and Amy swore she flirted with Paul in front of her.

Grudgingly, Amy knew Lucy brought important information about what was going on in the Appalachian Mountains. After she arrived, she told the elders about a group she called "the soldiers." She'd heard and seen them around Boone sometimes, but they didn't hang around long. They were all business. She described hearing heavy gunfire in the mountains, the sounds of battle. When it happened more than once, she decided to leave Boone and try to find a safer place. She had no other family. But she integrated into the community well.

Except when she pushed Amy's buttons regarding Paul.

When Paul came back from that foraging trip, he brought a ring. Amy absent-mindedly fingered that ring hanging round her neck. Paul gave it to her last Christmas, and he proposed to her in a little note he included in the gift box.

Amy flushed just thinking about it. She hadn't given her answer yet. She was just seventeen, going on eighteen. She knew she loved Paul and wanted to marry him. But they were so young. Before The Troubles, she had plans for college and a career. Maybe she would include marriage and a family a little further down the road. Now, though, things were very different. There was no college. The world was a mess. The best career she could hope for at this point was babysitting, gardening, and teaching others what she knew of martial arts.

She also wasn't sure how she felt about having children now. Life was hard, and it was going to get harder. Much as they worked to make things as normal and safe as possible in the community, there was only so much they could expect. The children she cared for at the school could expect about an eighth grade education, at best. The demands of life and survival would pull them out of the school by the time they were twelve or thirteen to help with family gardens, flocks, and herds. Most would also end up in the community security force, managed by Brad Anderson and James Carson.

#

"Hi, Amy."

That voice! Amy looked up and saw Lucy. She reached deep inside and pulled out her best smile. "Hi, Lucy."

"Shopping day, eh?" Lucy shifted her own pack on her back.

Amy looked around, realizing she had walked all the way to the open market in a fog.

"Yeah." Amy reached into her pack and pulled out a list her mom had left her this morning.

"Mind if I keep you company?"

"No, I guess not."

The first thing on Amy's list was lettuce. She didn't have a lot of fresh produce from her own family's garden for trade, as they ate most of what they produced. What she had were some potatoes, dry gourds from last year, various fresh and dried herbs.

"Let's see what they have for produce," Amy said. Lucy nodded, and they started across the market.

Yes, she found some lettuce. Leaf lettuce, both dark and light green. That would satisfy her mom's requirements, she thought. Amy was able to get a nice beef roast and some winter carrots for fewer bags of fresh and dried herbs than she thought she'd need.

All the time, she and Lucy chatted about life, the products available, and what the trades were worth. Amy started to feel a little guilty for her jealousy. She had a grudging, but growing liking for Lucy, in spite of the little green monster of jealousy rolling around in her gut.

After shopping, they went their separate ways home to store the food. Amy felt a pang of guilt knowing that Lucy went home alone and Amy got to go home to her family. As happy as Lucy seemed most of the time, Amy knew she was lonely.

When she got her supplies home, Amy had to run to the perimeter watch meeting and got there just in time.

Perimeter watch meetings were normally short and followed by specific training identified by either Brad Anderson or James Carson. They often tasked Amy with working with the watch participants on hand-to-hand combat techniques. Some in the watch started carrying bōs as Amy did, and were getting pretty good with them.

The community had only been attacked twice since the trip to Washington, D.C., and both times they beat the attackers back. That was largely thanks to the weapons cache found by the mission and the training and supervision of Brad and James. Amy preferred the bō to guns, but appreciated that they needed to keep an enemy at a distance.

On perimeter watch they used binoculars, and most of the time they found people coming to the community for help and safety. The community turned no one away so long as they were willing to contribute.

"Not much new," Brad said when everyone was seated. "When Lucy arrived, we started some recon patrols west of the community. So far, nothing new or threatening is out there. Even the gangs from other cities in the area—Winston-Salem and Charlotte—aren't showing any activity. We don't have any direct evidence, but we suspect they may have starved out or died from disease after this last hard winter."

"We'll keep an eye on things to the north and south, but we want to put some extra eyes on the west side observation posts now," James said. "We don't know who these 'soldiers' are, or who they were fighting, but if things spill this direction, we want to be ready."

Brad started handing out sheets of paper.

"These are the new watch schedules. The main changes have been on the west side O-Ps. We've added more cycles and watchers." Brad handed out the last of the sheets. "The main thing. We remember our training, keep to the schedules, report promptly, and move quietly. The entire community depends on us."

Amy looked at her schedule. They added another day to her watch duty and all but one of her watches were on the west side. She took a deep breath. The room started to buzz as the watch people started whispering about the changes.

"There's another change," James said, bringing the room to quiet again. "A number of you will have trainees going along with you." He raised his right arm and waved a group forward. "These are your trainees. They have been pre-assigned to watchers and will stay with those assigned watchers until we rotate them."

Sarah Shannon, Paul's little sister, moved up and sat next to Amy.

"I'm your trainee!" she said.

Surprised, Amy looked at Sarah, who was looking up and smiling broadly. Sarah's hair was an uncontrolled mane of soft black curls framing her tan face and hazel eyes. She was in shorts, a t-shirt, and sneakers.

"Uh," Amy wasn't sure what to say. She looked at the schedule again, then back at Sarah. "Okay, we have a watch tomorrow." She looked Sarah over, then decided. "We need to sort out some things with you before you go out on watch."

"Are you going to teach me to use the bō?"

"Probably, but not right away. First, we have to make you ready to go out. I think we need to get your hair tamed, then get you some better clothing."

"A real makeover, eh?"

"Oh, a makeover all right." Amy smiled and took Sarah's hand. The watch was dismissed, so they left the building and headed back to Amy's house. There, Amy dug through her old clothes to find something that would fit Sarah. A pair of cargo jeans, a long-sleeve t-shirt, and a pair of low-top hiking boots were the result.

"These are *old*," Sarah whined.

"That's not going to work with me, Sarah," Amy said. "I don't do whine. Change into these and we'll work on the hair next."

"What's wrong with my hair?" Sarah pulled on the cargo jeans.

"It's beautiful," Amy said. "But, it is all over the place. You'll end up getting it caught in everything, and you'll start finding strange things stuck in it after watch shifts."

"Like what?"

"Twigs, leaves, bugs ..."

"Big deal."

"Spiders."

Sarah's eyes went wide. "Okay."

Amy ran a brush through Sarah's thick curls and pulled the hair back. She tied it back and showed Sarah how to do it. After a couple of iterations of getting her hair under control, Amy thought Sarah was looking more ready for watch.

"Stand in front of the mirror, there," Amy said, pointing to a spot on the floor in front of the mirror. "Look at yourself."

Sarah did as requested.

"When we go on watch, this is how you should look." Amy handed her a denim jacket. "If it is cold, or we'll be out after dark, bring this."

"I look different," Sarah said, turning a little one way then the other.

"Yep, little girl. You're starting to grow up."

Amy waved Sarah over to a chair.

"Here's the watch schedule. Our first one is tomorrow. I'll come by and pick you up about a half hour before it starts. We have some gear to pick up before we go out to the first O-P."

"This is exciting!"

Amy wrote a note, folded it and gave it to Sarah.

"Give this to your mom, Sarah. This is important. She needs to get you up early and make sure you get breakfast and have some lunch packed."

Sarah unfolded the note and read it.

"Four-thirty? In the afternoon?"

"No, Sarah. Four-thirty in the morning. That's when I'll be by to pick you up."

#

Later, as Amy worked with Paul in his family's garden, she studied him from the side for a moment. He tried to keep his hair short and the soft black curls held close to his head. He had his mother's nose, and his father's chin. She knew he still ran every chance he could, and would sometimes goad others into races at the old high school track. He wasn't as fast on the long mile as he was a couple of years ago, but he still had no competition in the community. His shoulders and arms were larger, as was his chest.

Paul amazed her at what he could lift and how hard he worked at everything he did. Over the last couple of years, she witnessed the change of a boy coming into manhood. He was so different from the skinny boy who used to chase her around the beach when the families would vacation on the Outer Banks.

Now, when he wrapped his arms around her, she felt secure and just a bit scared. He was so strong. An unthinking move could hurt her. But Paul was always so gentle with her.

"Hey," Paul said suddenly, "quit daydreaming and get busy. We have to get these carrots planted, and then plant another frame of lettuce."

That jerked Amy out of her thoughts, but she saw a smile on Paul's face. She smiled back and brushed a wisp of hair out of her eyes.

"Okay, bully," she said and started putting carrot seeds in a shallow trench in the soft, black dirt.

TWO

Sarah

A hellhound and her puppies charged Amy. She tried to find the line of salt that made a barrier but couldn't.

"Paul!" She called for him, but she couldn't find him. She tried to spin her bō, but it felt like she was moving in molasses. The hellhound kept getting closer, and one of the pups was trying to bite her leg.

"Paul," she cried out once again.

Amy jerked awake.

Too early, she thought. Fragments of the dream that brought her to wakefulness drifted away with the lightening sky from early dawn outside her bedroom window. She turned and tried to go back to sleep, but her mind continued to race and threw memories of last year's mission into her now fully awake mind. Images of hellhounds and a demon trampled on her sleep all too often lately. She looked at the clock.

She gave up. A shower would get her ready for the day, and she had to pick up Sarah at 4:30. She got up and went into the bathroom.

#

Watch went better than Amy expected. Sarah took everything seriously, listened, practiced, and followed Amy's instructions. Amy suspected Sarah got some coaching at home the night before. They went over radio procedures extensively during the watch, and Sarah even got to make a few reports before they were done.

"O-P, Observation Post," Sarah mumbled to herself as she sat next to Amy in the O-P looking through the binoculars. "Contact, that's something we see, but we're not sure exactly what it is. Could be a deer or bear. Or, a person."

"You're getting it, Sarah," Amy said. "Now, our watch is ending. In the next few minutes, we'll get a signal from our replacements on the radio. Our replacements will already be at the next O-P. That means we can leave and go home."

"So, they don't come here to replace us?"

"No, they go to the next one. Just like we did when we started. No one was there. We radio'd the watchers we replaced. They were in another O-P." Amy's arm indicated a direction off to her left. "Then every fifteen minutes through our watch, we moved to a new O-P."

"Why do we do that?"

"It keeps us from getting sleepy and gives us fresh views every few minutes. It's something Carson came up with. Some like it, some don't. But, it seems to work well."

"It seems kinda silly to me."

"You'll see the wisdom at some point," Amy said. "Your brother likes it, too."

Sarah frowned.

The radio chirped. "O-P 10 secure. Jones out."

Amy keyed her radio. "Roger. Grossman out." Then she looked at Sarah.

"And that's it," Amy said grabbing her gear. "Let's go."

#

Near the market, Amy sent Sarah home with encouraging words about her efforts in the watch.

She is so young, Amy thought. It was hard to look back on herself at that age, even though it wasn't that long ago. Sarah seemed more disconnected, untethered. Amy had Paul and Joe as she grew up, and they were inseparable. Sarah had a few friends, but none as close as Amy, Paul, and Joe were. She had little Roger at home, but he was a little brother and more of a distraction for her than anything. Paul, of course, doted on her when he was around. But, that's what big brothers did.

Vendors and helpers set up the market for the day as Amy approached. Just mid-morning, it seemed strange that the rest of the community was just getting their day started when she was well into her own.

She knew Paul worked with the security forces today, and made checks on the perimeter watch throughout the day. She probably wouldn't see him until much later. So, now she had a little time to herself. She turned toward the community hall.

The community hall served as town hall, church, meeting hall, and hosted community festivals and celebrations. Elder Ray Franklin stood on the porch taking in the Carolina sun. Just who Amy wanted to see. Elder Franklin led the mission to Washington, D.C. last year. Amy and Paul depended heavily on him for guidance and support during that time.

Amy smiled as she approached him. It seemed his bushy mane of hair and eyebrows were whiter and larger than ever, always contrasting with his darker skin and gentle, deep brown eyes.

"Hi, Elder Franklin!"

"Good morning, Amy. Looks like you've been on watch already today."

"Just got off," she said as she stepped up to the porch. She took a deep breath. "Can we talk?"

"I always have time for you, my dear," Elder Franklin said giving her a sideways hug. He waved at the swinging chair hanging in the shade at the end of the porch. "Let's have a seat."

The swinging chair had plenty of room for both of them and cushions to make it comfortable.

"I saw you and Lucy shopping in the market yesterday," Elder Franklin began, his dark eyes twinkling. "I could swear I saw a friendship growing there."

Amy opened her mouth to respond, then closed it and thought a moment. Lucy joined the community just before Christmas, and the green fire of jealousy burned bright in Amy's heart ever since. She'd prayed about it, asked God to help her with it. Even though Paul didn't seem to pay that much attention to Lucy, Amy still burned.

"That's what I wanted to talk about." She folded her hands in her lap, then shifted to look more directly at the elder. "I don't know what to do about Lucy. When I'm with Paul, and she's around, I get all wound up inside. I know I'm jealous. I know she's sweet on Paul, and I think she flirts with him a lot. I don't think Paul has a clue, though."

Elder Franklin smiled and chuckled softly.

"Oh, I think Paul is pretty settled in this regard." He pointed at Amy's chest where the ring hung. "He gave you that ring for a reason. He made that decision during the trip that brought Lucy back with him. To Paul, Lucy is just a friend."

"I keep trying to tell myself that."

"Jealousy is a strong emotion, Amy." Elder Franklin nodded. "You have to deal with it or it will tear you apart. It can destroy your relationship with Paul, too. Making Lucy a friend will help, but you have to deal with that jealousy."

"How? Every time I see her, talk to her, think about her, I get all ... twisted up."

"Well, first you have to examine the emotion. You have to find the root cause. Sometimes, there are other reasons for what we feel than what you see on the surface. Jealousy can have roots in guilt, anger, or other negative feelings. You, Paul, and Joe were longtime friends growing up. You may have developed assumptions about your life, your friends, your future, based on that long-term relationship. Joe is now gone. Both you and Paul have a hole in your life as a result. There might be something there that you don't see that is now manifesting itself as jealousy of Lucy."

Amy's eyes were wide now. This could be more complicated than she thought.

"I see my words having an impact."

"Yeah, you're giving me something to think about. Something I haven't considered before." All she saw inside now was a swirly morass of feelings and thoughts. She couldn't, right now, pick out any one thing to focus on. She felt her eyes filling with tears.

"Well, we should do more than think about it. Lucy truly needs a good friend. Amy knows how to be a good friend. I know that to be a fact. Can I pray for you, Amy?"

"Yes, Elder Franklin," Amy said. She bowed her head and her tears overflowed and dripped from her eyes.

"Father," Elder Franklin began. He put a hand on Amy's shoulder. "I come to you on behalf of my dear friend and little sister, Amy, who struggles with negative feelings. You know her heart, Father. She has been a soldier for you in the past, and we know she will always be faithful. Please help her understand her feelings and help her resolve the negative feelings so she can move forward in a positive way."

He took a deep breath, paused in silence for a bit, then continued.

"We ask this in the name of your beloved son, Jesus Christ. Amen."

"Amen," Amy repeated. She wiped her face with her sleeve. She felt calmer, but still confused.

THREE

Stranger

Amy dug around in her emotions.

Guilt, anger. As usual, Elder Franklin hit a truth. Something she hadn't been thinking about. What had she buried that would make jealousy such a strong surface emotion?

She mulled this over on the way to the gym. A good, hard workout often helped her clear her mind.

The high school now served mostly as a community resource for child care, meetings, work spaces. The gym still served as a gym, but not just for students. Amy changed into her gi and claimed an open space on the gym floor to work in.

She started with her non-weapon katas, working her way up from Taikyoku, Helan, and Tekki and into her advanced katas. The legs and sleeves of her gi snapped sharply with punches and kicks as she moved around the floor. The walls echoed from her cries as she released.

Then, she picked up her bō and worked through several weapons katas with it. The gym walls again echoed with snaps and bangs as the bō hammered on the floor and whipped into attacks.

She finished with a soothing set of movements she had developed to help release tension and cool down. This ended with her folded on her knees, forehead to the floor, and praying to God.

"Thank you, God, for the strength and ability to do this. Help me to be the person you need me to be. All glory to you and your son, Jesus. Amen."

She remained in the position, her forehead on the cool floor, the bō next to her.

"I don't think I realized—until now—how very dangerous you are."

Amy jumped from her prayer position to an attack stance with the bō slanting toward the source of the voice.

A brief look of fear passed across Lucy's face. Then she laughed and started dribbling a basketball.

"I was going to see if you wanted to shoot some hoops, then I saw what you were doing and watched. That was incredible."

Amy relaxed and slowly, gently, pulled the bō to her side.

"I usually ignore whoever is in the gym when I work out," Amy said. "Too much distraction otherwise."

"So, you want to play a little one-on-one? Or, are you too tired?" Lucy, still bouncing the ball, gave Amy a challenging grin.

Amy set her bō down with her other gear.

"Oh, I think I can go for fifteen points. Half-court over here?"

"Sure. I have to warn you. I'm Cherokee. We play 'rez' basketball. It's a full contact sport, ya know."

Amy smiled accepting the challenge. "Okay."

Lucy took it out first and brought the ball to just above the key. She shot, and it bounced off the rim. Amy picked up the rebound and dribbled back toward Lucy.

"Shooting like a Duke," Amy said, grinning.

"It's on, lady," Lucy said and went into an aggressive defense.

Amy played her best and answered the rough and tumble Lucy brought with her own physical play. Elbows, knees, and hips clashed, and shots were blocked, missed, and made. Neither gave ground, and both charged full on. Had the game been refereed, Lucy thought, both would have been ejected in the first few minutes. But the game ground on.

Amy, sweat pouring down her face, brought the ball in and feinted left, then charged right. She ducked an elbow, then went up for the shot. Lucy's hand reached to block just short, and the ball bounced off the backboard and into the hoop.

"Fifteen, fourteen," Amy said after grabbing the ball, then sat on the floor. "I win."

"You cheated," Lucy said, collapsing next to her.

"So did you."

Both started laughing. Amy, exhausted, rolled onto her back. Lucy fell over with her head on Amy's shoulder.

"That was fun," Lucy said when she could catch her breath.

"Yeah." Amy managed to get her breathing under control and tenderly touched her ribs on the right side. "But, it hurts when I laugh."

"I warned you. Full contact."

"Don't make me laugh again."

Back in her regular clothes after a shower, Amy felt alive and human again. Still, the ribs were tender, but it was just a bruise.

"How did you learn all that fighting stuff?" Lucy tied her hair back and checked the locker room mirror for a small bruise on her chin.

"I took karate since I was about eight."

"Who was your teacher?"

"He was a really neat guy, married. He was one of the people we lost in the mission to Washington, D.C."

"So, are you teaching others?"

"Well, no, not officially. I help the watch and security force with some techniques. But, no, I'm not qualified to be a sensei."

"Could'a fooled me."

"Some of that you saw was never taught in our classes. I learned some things in the last couple of years and had to develop some techniques."

"I heard something about hellhounds."

"Yeah, that was one of the reasons. I don't think hellhounds were in the minds of the karate masters when they developed the katas."

"Isn't Zen pretty tightly integrated with the karate or martial arts?"

"It can be. I'm a Christian, though. So, I leave out the Zen part."

Amy looked at Lucy a moment. This was the most relaxed she'd been with the person she considered her competition for Paul. Right now, though—sore ribs and all—she felt a kinship with her. Maybe Elder Franklin was right. There is a friendship developing.

"I feel a little embarrassed," Amy said. "You've taken the lead twice now to try to make friends with me, and I haven't been very open to it."

"I like you, Amy," Lucy said. "I want us to be friends. To be honest, I'm pretty alone here." She tugged a little on the cord holding the ring. "I think you are the luckiest girl in the world. You just don't know it."

Amy looked down. She was talking about Paul, Amy knew that. It bothered her a little. She looked back up at Lucy.

"We're so young, yet," Amy pulled the ring out and looked at it. "I just don't know what to do."

"Look, I know he asked you to marry him. I don't think he's in a hurry or anything, but it would be good to give him an answer."

"What do you know about it?"

"Amy, from the time I met Paul, and he brought me to the community, I noticed one thing about him. You are in his thoughts all the time. Every time we stopped on the road, he'd have the box with that ring out and looking at it. I just remember thinking that I wish I had a guy who loved me that much."

"Really?"

"Really. Yeah, I flirted with him a bit, but he's kinda dense and just didn't see I was interested. I think I know why he loves you, now. You're tough, if a little possessive." Lucy gave her a sideways grin. "But you're a good friend, his best friend."

"But, this world ..."

"Look, lady, this is the world we have now." Lucy shifted her pack on her shoulder as they left the building. "For our lifetimes, there's no college, no careers, no going off to the big city for glamorous jobs. Maybe not for our grandkids lifetimes. All that is off in the far future now. We have to make our lives here and now."

Amy stood out in the sun for a moment enjoying the warmth and looking at Lucy.

"You have nothing to worry about with me, Amy. I just want a friend, and you are the best possible candidate."

"I think I see that." Amy reached out to hug Lucy. Lucy hugged her back.

"That's better." Lucy pulled back and looked at Amy.

"Yeah."

#

Amy watched the approaches to the community from her hidden position. She was in a prepared, camouflaged observation post located on her perimeter watch route. Sarah sat next to her shadowing Amy's activities. She came along to learn the process. Now eleven—almost twelve—years old, Sarah could help with the patrols, observing, and reporting.

Amy thought Sarah would soon have a perimeter watch of her own and would be a good companion on foraging patrols. But they were sending fewer and fewer foraging patrols out. The foragers had to go further and further from the community to find useful items and safe food. The community grew to be more and more self-reliant, growing or producing almost every need.

"Something is moving out there, Amy," Sarah whispered as she looked away from her binoculars. She pointed in the direction she was looking and returned to looking through her binoculars.

Amy brought up her binoculars and looked. *Yes*, she thought, *something is moving*.

"Good job, Sarah. It's time to change position, anyway," Amy whispered. "Let's go to the next O-P. We'll get a better view of whatever is moving out there."

"Okay," Sarah said, smiling as she picked up her small pack and staff.

Amy slung her pack on, grabbed her staff and led the way out of the observation post.

Keep moving, stay alert, stay hidden, were the words that rolled through her head as she walked quietly down the trail across the reverse slope of the ridge. James Carson, the community's process expert, would repeat those words frequently in training the perimeter watch. He is the one who thought up the concept that the watch would only sit in an O-P for fifteen minutes, then move to another. Each O-P had overlapping fields of observation with the other O-P's. Brad Anderson—a vet and one of the people Amy and Paul worked with in Washington, D.C. during the mission almost two years ago—kept referring to it as "overlapping fields of fire." Brad's primary responsibility was training the community defenses. Since the return from the mission, the community had to defend itself from attacks by gangs and bandits. The "overlapping fields of fire" concept saved the community more than once.

At the next O-P, Amy got Sarah set up, and they found the 'something moving' again. It turned out to be a 'someone' moving along one of the roads approaching the community.

Amy keyed her radio.

"HQ, Patrol three," she said, "we have a contact on the southwest road. Continuing to observe. Over."

"Patrol three, HQ, roger, out."

Amy handed the radio to Sarah.

"I'll keep an eye on the contact, you relay on the radio."

"Okay," Sarah said. Amy could hear the excitement in Sarah's voice.

Amy focused on the contact as it slowly approached. It was still about a half-mile out, so she couldn't tell if it was male or female. He or she was walking along the side of the road, rather than down the middle. As it drew closer, she could tell it carried a weapon and held it as if prepared to use it at any moment.

"Patrol three, HQ. Squad dispatched to your location. Over." The radio chirped. The volume was on low, so Amy barely heard the communication.

"HQ, Patrol three, roger. Patrol three on schedule. Out." Sarah looked over at Amy.

Basically, reporting that their patrol was on schedule told HQ exactly where they were, so Amy was certain the squad being dispatched knew where to meet them. Amy nodded back to Sarah and went back to her binoculars.

The contact continued its slow approach. Amy could finally make out that the contact was heavily armed, very likely a male, and moved as if expecting trouble at any moment.

"It looks like a soldier," Amy whispered.

"Didn't Lucy mention something about soldiers in the Appalachian Mountains?"

"Yeah," Amy replied. *Lucy*, she thought. Her inner turmoil rose to the surface, and she had to take a breath and calm herself. Things were better, but she still needed to deal with the roots of her jealousy.

"Why do you always do that when someone says Lucy's name?"

"Do what?"

"Look really mad, then take a deep breath."

Just then, the radio chirped twice.

"Come in," Amy said, relieved for the interruption.

The squad leader moved into the O-P. Amy pointed where the soldier moved, and the squad leader looked through his own binoculars.

"Okay," he said, "We'll move to intercept. Hope this doesn't turn into a shooting fest."

"Me, too," Amy said. The squad leader disappeared into the brush, and Amy could barely hear the rest of the squad move out.

#

Amy and Sarah reported to the community hall after their watch. A lot of people were in and around it. Amy suspected word had spread quickly about the soldier that showed up.

At the front of the large meeting room, Brad and James sat next to the stranger, and Elder Franklin was getting ready to talk.

"Looks like we got back just in time," Amy whispered to Sarah.

Elder Franklin cleared his throat and faced the room.

"Friends," he said, "we have some startling information. It seems that more of Satan's work from more than two years ago is revisiting us. If I hadn't heard about what happened in Asheville before—from our own Amy and Paul—I might not have believed what this young man just told us.

"Asheville, during The Troubles, was overrun by zombies. According to our young visitor," the elder waved his hand at the soldier, "a group of National Guard accessed the local armory and started a campaign of containment. They tried to keep the zombies confined to the Asheville area. Unfortunately, the zombie infection seeped away into the surrounding mountain communities, and the numbers increased.

"I swear, it seems as if I'm in an old horror movie right now. Who would have thought we'd have to deal with zombies?"

He turned to the soldier.

"Would you please introduce yourself, and give us a status of the conflict?"

"Thank you, Elder. Yes."

The solider stood and faced the room.

"I'm Sergeant Ronald Flynn, platoon sergeant of Second Platoon, Company C, 201 Battalion, Mountain Infantry, North Carolina National Guard. Well, what's left of it, anyway. We had a full company of mountain infantry when this started. We are down to just two platoons now, and a weapons section.

"Until last summer, we were able to keep the bulk of the zombies contained in the Asheville area. Unfortunately, we were getting low on resources. We sent squads to other towns we knew had armories to try to get more ammunition and weapons. We had some success, but the diversion of troops allowed more zombies to wander into neighboring areas. More zombies appeared and in rapidly increasing numbers."

He looked around the room.

"Yes, if you get bitten or ingest some of their fluids, you get turned into a zombie. I don't know if Satan used our own fears to create this mess, or if it was some disease that lay dormant for centuries. But, we have it now. And, like you may have heard in horror movies or read in books, the only way to take one down is a head shot. It doesn't matter if you use a bullet or a baseball bat, the head is your target. If you have a problem with the concept, think if it as mercy. You are freeing some poor soul from a horrible existence.

"The zombie horde is growing and moving. And it is moving this direction. We currently have it stopped at a line from Old Fort to Mill Spring. But, since we don't have the horde contained, they are able to roam north and south and increase their numbers."

The silence in the room was deafening.

Paul stood, and Amy felt a swell of pride when she saw him. Paul was eighteen, but looked physically as mature and well-constructed at Sgt. Flynn.

"Sgt. Flynn," Paul said, "how long did it take you to get here from your unit?"

"Six days," Flynn said. "I came as fast as I could."

Paul nodded. Amy knew Paul's foraging patrols had gone as far as Shelby, so he knew how long it could take on foot.

"So, a lot may have changed since you left?"

"My last radio contact was two days ago. They were still holding that line then. I can't speak to what may have happened since then, I'm afraid."

"How well equipped and supplied is your unit now?" Brad asked.

"We're in good shape. But, we don't have many vehicles or extra weapons or ammo. Food is okay. MRE's. They last for years, you know."

Chuckles and laughs from veterans spread across the room.

James stood and hung a large map of North Carolina on the wall.

"We have some weapons and a good enough supply of ammo for defense of the community against a raiding party, gang or similar threat. However, this is very different," James said. He pointed to a location near Raleigh, then another near Durham.

"There are armories in these two locations. While the units they used to support are not infantry, there should be stocks of weapons and ammo that would help."

"And I now have extensive experience in cracking opening the vaults," Sgt. Flynn said with a big, toothy smile.

"We would have to strip a large part of our community security and defense to help," James said. "But I think we can make the necessary arrangements. This is too big a threat to ignore."

"Well," Sgt. Flynn said, then sighed, "if we can't get this stopped ..."

"I think we get the message," Brad said.

FOUR

Preparation

Amy and Paul watched—from a distance—as Sgt. Flynn pressed a blasting cap into the C4 explosive formed around the lock and frame of the heavy green armory vault. They then carefully followed the ignition wires back to the front of the building. Brad, James, and members of the community security force crouched behind concrete walls.

"Ready," Sgt. Flynn said as he crouched down next to Brad. Flynn retrieved a wire from Brad and twisted it around a terminal on a small switch. He got the other wire from James and twisted it around the other terminal on the switch.

"Fire in the hole. Fire in the hole. Fire in the hole," Flynn shouted, and everyone huddled smaller.

Then he pressed the switch. A loud thump sounded deep in the armory, the floor and walls shook, and a cloud of dust pushed out of doors and windows. Then there was a loud clang.

"I think that clang was the vault door," Flynn said.

"I expected a lot of fire and smoke," Paul said.

"That was Hollywood," Brad said. "This is reality."

"I don't like to use explosives on the vaults," Flynn said. "There is a risk of secondary explosions depending on what might be stored in there. But it's the most expedient. C4 is powerful, but controllable."

"What are we waiting for?"

"Any secondary explosions, Paul," Flynn replied. "Give it a few more seconds. Then we go in."

When they did go inside, the armory door lay on the floor. Amy could see smoke rising from the edges where the C4 cracked through the thick steel.

"Don't touch the door," Flynn warned. "Step around it. It's hot."

Weapons in racks stood in rows, and ammunition boxes were stacked in the back of the vault.

"Jackpot," Amy said.

"That sums it up," James agreed.

"Let's get loaded up," Brad said. He started directing the rest of the security force into the armory.

They loaded everything needed into three trucks from the armory yard.

Flynn had Amy and Paul help search through the vault and armory for any additional explosives or supplies.

"Look for things like green baseballs. Grenades. And anything that looks like a small rocket," he held up his hands about a foot apart, "about this size."

"What are the small rockets?" Amy asked.

"Mortars. Our weapons section is getting low on them. They are great at slowing the horde down."

"Okay," Paul said.

#

They repeated the process at the armory in Durham. This one didn't yield as much, but they found a lot of Meals Ready to Eat (MREs) that still had a few years before expiration.

"We have three deuce-and-a-halfs, fully fueled and ready," James said when they gathered in the hall back in the community. "And we found more than enough food, weapons, and ammo to equip our own people and supply C Company. We also have military radios and other equipment to help with the effort. What took Sgt. Flynn six days will take us about four to six hours to get linked up with C Company."

Amy looked at Paul. He reached over and held her hand and gave her a little smile.

"We are basically going to add two platoons to C Company," Brad said, moving to the front of the group. "I will lead one. We're calling it Fourth Platoon. Paul will head up Fifth Platoon. We roll out in an hour. Go home, get geared up, get some real food. Hug your families."

Amy and Paul left together.

"This is going to put a strain on our families," Amy said as they trotted toward their homes. "Mom and Dad will have to do all the chores we've been doing."

"They'll deal," Paul said. He slowed to a walk as they approached the little wooden foot bridge into their neighborhood. "Sometimes, I look back on what happened back then and it's hard to believe we were so young and carried such burdens."

"At least there are no trolls," Amy said.

Paul stopped her on the bridge and turned toward her. He was very close. Amy's heart pounded, and her hands shook.

"We'll get through this, Amy," he said. "No matter what. And, you know I love you."

She smiled and looked up at him, and he was right there and kissed her. Her stomach started doing flip-flops, and her arms went around his neck. The kiss ended, and he slowly pulled away.

"We have a lot to do," he said.

"I know. I'll see you back at the hall." She turned and ran home. She felt as if she flew home.

#

Amy packed her backpack with clothes and necessities. Most of the supplies she'd need would be on the trucks. Food, weapons, ammo. Personal things she needed she had to bring. She had no idea how long this would be. It was summer in North Carolina, so she didn't need heavy clothing. The boots and camouflage gear they scavenged from the armories were more than tough enough for outer wear.

Plan for a month, she told herself. She stuffed more underwear and socks in the large compartment.

The weapons they would use were the M4 carbines. Amy didn't like guns much. She'd trained on them with the security force, and she could hit what she aimed at. The thought of head shots caused a bit of a roll in her tummy, though. The small telescopic sight on the M4 got you up close on the target. She cringed a little at the thought.

"Well, it can't be worse than killing hellhound puppies," she said to herself.

She reached for her bō, then stopped. If the zombies got close enough the carbine was no longer effective, and she needed another weapon, a pistol or ... her eyes shifted to the box in her closet where she kept her other karate weapons.

Sai.

The metal forks, with a long center tang, made excellent offensive and defensive tools for close in fighting. She grabbed the pair of sai and slipped the long tangs into loops on the sides of her backpack.

Perfect, she thought sarcastically. *I'm getting into a cold-blooded killer mindset.*

It disturbed her that techniques to effectively use the sai against zombies, specifically getting the center tang through the head, rolled through her mind. Granted, she'd practiced the katas for sai. The movements and spinning of the sai through the forms was elegant and graceful. And deadly. She hoped they would keep her alive if it came to using them.

On the way out of the house, after a light meal, she hugged her mom and dad.

"I'll be careful," she said and hurried out. She had no idea what would come, but she didn't want her parents to see the tears coming in her eyes. If her mom had seen, she would have started a crying fest, and Amy may never have gotten away.

The jog back to the hall helped clear her mind. The last couple of years gave her experience in just going forward and not looking back. She had to trust God had a plan for her and not worry. *Be faithful*, she told herself.

"But, I worry about zombies," she said aloud. "Please, God, protect me from zombies."

FIVE

Link Up

Five hours in the back of a military truck bouncing down the highway was not at the top of Amy's list of fun things to do. She didn't think it would even make the list. It was hot, loud, and smelly. Too many sweaty bodies packed in around the ammo crates.

She and Lucy spent a lot of time talking, and that made the trip a little bearable at least. Amy wished for some time with Paul, but he was in one of the other trucks. Fortunately, so was Sgt. Flynn. His absence allowed Lucy to talk openly.

"He is so cute," Lucy said. "I got to talk to him a little. Elder Franklin had him over to his house for dinner, and I got invited." Lucy wiggled with excitement. "He's very nice. Unattached. Oh, he has the nicest smile."

"How old is he?"

"I think he said twenty-five. I didn't catch all of that part of a conversation. I'm almost twenty, so we're close." Lucy smiled and hugged herself. Amy thought she looked pleased and at peace.

Amy had difficulty imagining herself at twenty-five. A few years ago, that seemed so old. Now, she was eighteen, her friend was close to twenty, and that friend was considering a boyfriend who was twenty-five. Somehow, she was approaching a life threshold where age became a non-issue. For so long, it seemed, the difference of a year was so ... huge. She, Paul, and Joe were just months apart in age, and that seemed to help bond them as friends.

"What," Lucy said, looked directly at Amy. "You think he's too old for me?"

"Oh, no," Amy pulled herself back to the present. "No, not at all. I was just thinking how things have changed so much. How my perception of age has changed."

"Oh, I see. Deep thoughts," Lucy laughed. "The Troubles have changed a lot of things. Before, I was thinking of college, a career, and maybe settling down with a family at about thirty or so. Now, I feel like I'll be an old maid if I don't get hitched before twenty-one. Like, what else is there?"

"Yeah," Amy agreed. "Life isn't that way anymore. There's no pressure for a career. No pressure to get an advanced education—much less any opportunity for that now. I keep wondering what else we might be doing, but I always come back to marriage, children, family, and surviving."

"Kinda simplified things, didn't it? The Troubles."

"In a way, yes."

#

At a rest stop, Brad called everyone together.

"We made radio contact with C Company. They've been pushed back. They're holding a line from Lake James on the north, to Cliffside and Henrietta to the south. We're planning to link up at Union Mills in about an hour. Once there, we probably won't have a lot of time for pleasantries. We'll get deployed right away and may even see action immediately.

"Lucy," Brad pointed to her, "is fourth platoon's sniper."

Lucy held up her modified M4 with the larger, longer scope.

"Joshua," Brad pointed to a young man standing next to Paul, "is fifth platoon's sniper. Snipers must get set up quickly and get clear fields of fire to the front. They'll help thin the hordes down from a distance."

"The weapons section is almost out of ammunition," Sgt. Flynn spoke up. "One of the first things off the trucks when we find the company HQ need to be the crates of mortar ammo. When we stop, two people per crate—not snipers—grab and run those crates to the weapons section. You'll be directed. Then you can get back to your units."

"Walk around and get some air," Brad said. "We roll again in ten."

Amy made her way over to Paul, who was talking with some of his troops. She waited patiently while he talked. He finally saw her and broke away and joined her.

"We haven't had much time together these last few days," he said.

"No, and I'm missing that." Amy fiddled with the ring hanging on the cord. "I think I need to tell you something."

"Oh?"

"Yes."

"What?"

"That was it." Amy felt the color rising through her neck and cheeks. "Yes."

"Yes what?"

She held the ring up in front of his face.

"Yes—this," she said. *Sometimes you can be so dense,* she thought.

Paul stared at the ring a moment, then threw his arms around Amy. He kissed her. She felt warm and fluid in his embrace, and her heart fluttered.

"What took you so long?" he asked as he finally let her go.

"I had a lot to think about. And now I know that marrying you is the most right, best thing I could ever do."

Paul seemed dumbstruck, but smiled at her.

"I don't think it will be right away, though," Amy said. "We still have some time, some things to do. Say, in six months or a year?"

"That would be fine with me," Paul said. "Any time would be fine with me. Tomorrow or the day after, even. But, you said 'Yes,' so that makes it official."

Truck horns sounded.

"I love you, Paul."

"Love you, too!"

On the way back to the truck, Amy saw Lucy talking to Flynn. Lucy's arms were folded behind her back. *That's how you keep from constantly touching him, I know,* Amy thought. She'd used that so many times to keep from touching or throwing her arms around Paul in public.

Lucy talked, laughed, and smiled up at Flynn. He seemed to be enjoying their time together. Then, Lucy tore herself away from him and headed for the truck.

#

"Maybe we'll have a double wedding," Amy told Lucy when they were back in the truck and bouncing down the road.

"Huh?"

"I saw you vamping Sgt. Flynn."

"He likes to be called Ron." Lucy hugged herself.

"That's what I thought."

"What?"

"I think you're sprung on him."

"Me, too." She sighed.

They chatted and sat quietly in turns for the next hour. As the time for the link up grew closer, Amy felt the tension from the rest of the troops in the truck. It was a reflection of the tension in herself. She practiced some breathing to help calm her nerves. Soon, she was checking her pack, the sai, her carbine, cleaning the little telescopic sight, checking her extra magazines.

Amy noticed Lucy started performing similar actions. She pulled her compound bow from a fabric case, checked it over, looked at the cams, and put a drop of oil in the axels of the cams and pulleys. Then she drew the bow several times to check the operation. She counted her arrows. Fifteen. She cleaned her sniper scope and checked the operation of her carbine and the status of her ammunition.

"Do you expect to use the bow much?" Amy asked, wiping her carbine down with a rag.

"No. But, I'll keep it handy. If I run out of ammo, it will be a last resort. Actually, I'm probably a better shot with the bow than the carbine. At medium ranges, anyway."

"It doesn't have a scope or sights, I notice," Amy said.

"I took the sights off. I don't use 'em," Lucy slid the bow back into the case. "I've always been a better natural shot with the bow. I never could get the hang of those sights."

Amy's behind took a few hard bounces on the wood slat bench as the truck turned and slowed.

"Ouch!"

"Yeah," Lucy agreed, laughing.

When they stopped, both stood and stretched. Lucy launched out of the back of the truck first. Amy and another trooper grabbed a handle on each side of a crate of mortars and followed directions to the weapons section. When they arrived with the crate, another member of C Company told them where to stack it. Amy set her side of the crate down, then looked at the small, portable mortar tubes spread across a yard behind a house.

"Get to your unit now," the trooper from C Company told her.

She retraced her steps and found Brad.

"Back in the truck," Brad said. "We're assigned the south flank. Let's go!"

There was more room in the truck now, with the mortar crates gone. Lucy was back, but had more information.

"We're going to try to anchor the south flank," she said. "I got to hang with Brad when he talked to the company commander."

A trooper next to Lucy asked, "What's a flank?"

Amy looked at him. He couldn't have been more than fifteen, maybe sixteen.

"It's the side or end of a line," she said and smiled at him. He nodded and smiled back.

"Thanks," he said. Then his face returned to the worried look most of the rest had.

Oh, man, Amy thought. *They're just children, most of them.*

"They are just kids," Lucy whispered, reading Amy's mind.

"That obvious what I was thinking?"

"Yep."

Another ten minutes or so, and the truck turned and stopped again.

Brad came around the back to let them out.

"Lucy, I have a spot for you," he said as he helped her out. See that garage? There. You can get on top from the back. Flat roof, and you can set up with a field looking west down this road."

"Got it." Lucy ran to the garage.

When the rest of the platoon assembled, Brad looked them over.

"Okay," he counted out seven troops and pointed to his right. "You over here." Then he directed the rest of the platoon to his left.

"Everyone face west."

They all did and looked down the road.

"This is the Harris-Henrietta Road. This will be our center. You on my right will spread north to the Dogwood Valley Golf Course. There's a power line right-of-way you can use for some of your movement. However, there is a bend in the Second Broad River that has no north-south bridges, so you'll have to work around that. Pay particular attention to Pepper Town Road, and make sure one of you is stationed looking west there.

"Those on my left will spread south from here down the Hog Pen Branch and Henry Jenkins Roads. We'll stretch as far as we can to the south. We are the anchor on the south here. Ricky," Brad put his hand on the trooper's shoulder, "is my radio operator and will keep us in contact with the company. You all have platoon radios in your helmets, so we can coordinate fire and movement. Turn them on now."

Amy picked up her helmet and looked for the radio. She turned it on and it crackled briefly. Then she put the helmet on. She adjusted the boom mic in front of her mouth.

"Up," she said. She heard others through the helmet report.

"Move out," Brad said through the radio.

Amy moved with the rest of her section to the south. One by one, troopers stopped at a likely place and set up facing west. Amy took the third position. There would be four more troopers to her south.

She was in the back yard of a house off Hog Pen Branch Road, just north of where Henry Jenkins Road split off. West was a lot of open fields and a power distribution line running west-north-west. She set up in some trees that gave her cover and started setting up her field of fire. She used the little telescopic sight to identify and mark ranges out to her front, and mark her left and right limits.

"Amy, set," she said into the radio when ready.

Others reported their status for a few minutes.

"Contact," Lucy said over the radio. Amy could hear the stress in her voice. "Range fifteen hundred. Moving slowly. I see about thirty. Right on the road."

"Roger, contact 1500. Out," Brad acknowledged.

Amy scanned her field. Her little scope was good for about five hundred meters. Lucy's was good for almost two thousand. She probably couldn't start engaging until targets were about two or three hundred meters out, but she could start seeing them a lot further away. Amy thought she could try shooting, using her little scope, at about one hundred fifty meters at best.

Since every shot needed to be a head shot to be effective, all the troops were basically snipers now. Some were longer range than others.

"Solo contact, two hundred meters," Lucy said. "Engaging." There was a pause. "Contact eliminated."

A few seconds later, Amy heard the rifle report echo across the land. She scanned her front again.

Good job, Lucy, Amy thought.

Sporadic reports of contacts started popping up on the radio. A few reports of contacts engaged brought Brad to the radio.

"OK, we're engaging. No more reports required unless you are being overrun. Do not wait until you are overrun to report."

There was a flurry of "Roger, out" reports, then the radio went quiet.

Amy scanned her front, then she saw something.

SIX

Combat

Amy looked through her little scope and scanned across her front. About a hundred zombie bodies scattered across the area about one hundred fifty meters out. They had arrived in small waves all afternoon, sometimes single zombies, sometimes several. Amy was able to take them out before they got closer than one hundred meters. She felt that was an accomplishment. As a result, her shoulder was getting sore.

Lucy's reports on the platoon radio indicated she had a lot of success at longer ranges. Amy could hear rifle fire to her south and north, but no one was panicking, and everyone seemed to be holding their ground.

The rotting bodies lay across the fields in the heat of the day. The growing aroma drifted toward Amy. They were animated corpses, of course, Amy told herself. They were gonna stink. She wished for some mentholated cream, remembering how it was used in the D.C. mission.

The sun was getting low in the sky, and Amy had to put down the sun visor on her helmet. This had both positive and negative elements. The sun was bright and hurt her eyes. The zombies, on the other hand, were silhouetted against the sun and that made them easier to hit.

She squeezed off another round and watched the zombie go down. That emptied her magazine. She popped it out and slapped in a fresh one, then charged the weapon. She checked her pouches.

"I'm down to one more maggie," she called on the radio.

"I could use a resupply, too," another trooper reported. This was followed up and down the line by similar reports.

"Resupply will be along soon. Until then, make every shot count," Brad's voice crackled on the radio.

Amy looked through her scope again. There were three more over on the right side of her zone. She engaged them. Then there were five more coming down the middle. She missed one and had to take a second shot. Then there were six more on the right and four more on the left.

As she was finishing off the last of the four on the left, ten more came out of the middle of her zone. Then she lost count so she just worked the carbine. She changed magazines and worked some more. Then the carbine was empty.

"I'm out and there's a lot of them coming to my position," Amy reported.

One of the troops to the south reported the same, adding, "I'm moving north. Going to be overrun."

Two other troops to the south reported they were leaving their positions. No one wants to get cut off, Amy thought.

"Amy! Here's some ammo," a trooper came up from behind her and made her jump. Fortunately, her rifle was empty.

"Grab the empty maggies," Amy yelled tossing a bag of empty magazines to the trooper as he left. She shoved fresh magazines into her pouches and rifle. A bag of full ones were still on the ground in front of her. Then she turned and started firing.

"Getting busy here," Amy reported on the radio. "Have extra ammo. If you're coming this way, join me."

"Almost there," someone replied.

"We need to hold this position until everyone south of me is clear," Amy radioed.

"Roger, that," Brad said.

The fields at Amy's front were filling with bodies of zombies and more zombies. The bodies made navigating the fields difficult for them, and many stumbled and fell several times. That gave Amy time to thin the ranks. Still, some were getting to about seventy-five meters before she could take them out. Amy just couldn't shoot fast enough.

"I'm here," a voice said. Amy heard him running up, so she wasn't surprised this time.

"Ammo's in the bag there," she pointed. "Load up and start working."

Amy glanced at the troop. It was the young boy she noticed from the truck. He wore his stress and fear on his face. She shot down three more zombies then turned to him.

"It's gonna be all right," she said. "We hold 'em here until everyone is clear, then we move back to the main unit."

He nodded as he slapped a magazine into his carbine and charged it.

As they fired, two more troops showed up, loaded ammo and got busy.

They were holding the zombies to about seventy-five meters. Amy noticed now that they just kept coming. There was no longer a left, center, and right. It was just a flood of zombies across the front.

"Wasn't there another troop down that way?" she asked those with her. The young troop looked around.

"Yeah, Gary. He was just south of my position. I thought he headed here first."

One of the other troops offered, "I didn't see anyone else coming this way."

Amy looked around. The ammo bag was now empty. She had three empty magazines at her feet.

"I have four mags left," she told the others. She fired at two zombies.

"I have three," the young trooper said.

"Three."

"Four."

Amy fired several more times, then changed out the empty magazine. Her shoulder was very sore. Each shot fired brought searing pain with it.

"Now, three." She shoved the empties into the bag. "Get your empties into the bag when you have a chance."

"We're getting near to overrun. Ammo is low, and we have one troop unaccounted for," Amy reported on the radio. "We're going to start moving back to the main body."

"Roger," Brad said. "Be advised there are solos all over the place."

"Roger, out."

Amy took the bag of empty magazines, zipped it up, and tossed it to the young troop.

"Hang on to that," she said. "We'll need those mags to resupply."

Amy fired twice more and dropped two more zombies.

"Let's move," she said. "Three-sixty perimeter. Boss said there are solos all over the place."

She pointed where she wanted everyone to go, and they started moving. A zombie shambled around the side of the house to their rear. A carbine dangled useless from its shoulder. The young troop stopped and fired.

"That was Gary," the troop said.

"We have him accounted for then," Amy said. "Run!"

#

Amy had heard the phrase "runnin' and gunnin'" from veterans of Southeast Asia. That's what they were doing. She and the other three troops ran down roads, across fields, through small copses of woods, and gunned down anything that got in their way. The young troop led, Amy kept to the left.

"Go right," she yelled, providing direction to the group as they charged north on Hog Pen Branch Road. She didn't want them losing direction.

The troop behind her fired back at a zombie that came out of a farmyard they had just passed. The troop on the right gunned down a zombie wandering out in a field on their right side.

"We're coming north on Hog Pen," Amy radioed. "Link up with us if you can."

"I see you," came a voice on the radio. "Heading to you. Don't shoot me."

The young trooper looked back at Amy, then pointed. A troop was running their direction from a farmhouse to the northwest. The young trooper shot a zombie moving out of the woods toward that other troop.

"We're not stopping, so come on," Amy radioed.

Now they had five.

"What's your status?" Amy yelled as the troop joined them. She scanned to the left as she talked.

"Two magazines left," he said. "I'm okay, but man they were getting close!"

"OK, help the rear guard," she said pointing to the rear of the small group.

A few minutes later, another troop radioed to link up.

"We're coming around the big bend on Hog Pen. Head there," Amy directed.

Okay, Amy thought, *that's six.*

"All accounted for," Amy radioed to Brad. "Coming up on Hog Pen."

"Roger, out," Brad said.

Amy heard a lot of rifle fire coming from up ahead.

"Switch to full auto," Brad radioed. "Get ready to rock and roll."

Amy toggled the fire selector on her carbine to full auto. The other troops did the same.

As they broke into the little Henrietta community, Amy saw the rest of the platoon fighting a desperate attempt to keep from being overrun. She brought her group up through the houses on the south side of Harris Henrietta Road, and they joined in the fight.

"Hold as best you can, and move slowly back to the truck," Brad radioed. "We're almost out of ammo."

"Roger," Amy said. She moved her troops to cover the retreat of the rest of the platoon. From the corner of her eye, she saw Lucy on top of the garage. The sniper rifle was slung on her back, and she had her bow out.

A zombie came shuffling from behind some trees near Amy. Before Amy could bring her carbine around, Lucy's arrow brought it down.

"Thanks, Lucy," Amy radioed. "Better get off of there now."

Amy's carbine locked open. Empty. She reached into her pouches for another magazine. Nothing.

"I'm out," she yelled at her troops. Two others yelled the same. "Okay, retreat slowly."

Amy pulled a bandana out of a pocket and tied it across her nose and mouth. The smell of gun smoke and rotting zombie hung thick in the air. She slung her carbine over her back and pulled out the sai. "If you're out, head for the truck," she yelled.

"I'm out," another troop yelled.

That left two troops firing. Amy stood between them spinning the sai in her hands as they moved slowly back toward the truck.

"Everyone is in," Brad radioed. "Come on, Amy."

"Roger," Amy waved the two troops to the truck. "Run!"

Amy turned and ran to the truck. Three zombies came out from behind a building to her right. She had no way to get past them without a fight. She turned and attacked the nearest with a quick thrust of the sai, spun and ended a second. Then the third went down from Lucy's arrow.

Amy ran up and jumped into the truck. The engine roared already, so as soon as she was in, they were rolling.

"Pull up the side curtains," Brad radioed. "There is a little more ammo in the back there. Keep the zombies away."

The troops distributed the remaining ammo and got the side curtains pulled up.

The truck rumbled down the road with an occasional shot fired from the back.

"Thanks for the help, Lucy," Amy said as they rested in the back. She wiped zombie juice off the sai with a dirty rag, then tossed the rag out the back of the truck.

"Glad to do it. But, those're arrows I'll never get back."

"Yeah. How many you got left?"

"Twelve."

Amy touched her right shoulder and winced.

"Ouch," she said. "That rifle has a kick."

She opened her cammo shirt a bit and pulled down on her t-shirt. A large, purple bruise covered her shoulder. Lucy exposed her shoulder and displayed a similar bruise.

"I think we're going to need some pads if we're going to keep this up," Lucy said. "I knew it hurt, but I was too focused to pay any attention until now."

"Adrenaline," Amy said. "We're gonna pay for this, I think."

#

When the platoon rejoined C Company, they fought in the growing dark from the truck as the rest of the company mounted vehicles, and the entire company sped away toward Polkville. Amy reported to Brad that Gary, one of the troops in her section was lost. She learned that Paul's platoon had lost two troops.

She and Lucy spent most of the way to Polkville sleeping and bouncing on the wooden seats. Amy took the blessing of a break when they climbed out of the truck in Polkville.

"We're going to try to hold a line here," C Company Commander John Wilkinson said to the gathered company in Polkville. "We'll stretch our platoons along South Mountain Scenery Road down to just west of Shelby on US 74. We have lots of good, open country for lanes of fire. I just wish we had more heavy firepower.

"At the rate the zombies move, we have several hours before we expect to see them. Get resupplied, get some downtime, some food, and a little rest. The platoons will move out to their areas in two hours."

"I'm going to spend a little time with Paul," Amy said.

"Well, I think you know what I'll be doing," Lucy said.

"Behave."

Lucy grinned as she left the assembly area and gave Amy a little finger wave. Amy was enjoying this growing friendship with Lucy. She was salty, but sweet, and helped Amy think through things. It was refreshing to have someone she could talk to—to share with—that wasn't a boy. *Er, man,* she corrected herself.

Paul looked tired and drawn when she found him. She'd seen him like that in the past. She put her left arm around him. He tried to hug her, but she winced away.

"Big bruise," she said, and opened her shirt a little to show him.

"Wow, yeah. You need some ice. Let's go see the medic."

"Good idea."

At the field aid station, the medic pulled a cold pack out of a small freezer.

"Yeah, we get this sometimes. Keep that on the shoulder for a couple of hours. It will help, but you'll want some padding. Try to hold the rifle tighter. That way it doesn't slam against your shoulder."

"Wish I'd thought of that," Amy said. "Thanks."

She and Paul walked around the abandoned town in the twilight.

"How are you doing, Paul?" she asked, looking up at him. That's something else different, she realized. She had to look up at Paul these days. There was a time she had been taller.

"Okay," he said. "Things got a little intense on our side. I wasn't sure we'd get out of there when the horde showed up."

"We had a similar experience."

Paul tapped one of the sai. "Did you have to use those?"

"Just at the end, getting to the truck. We were out of ammo."

"We keep shooting them and more keep coming," Paul said. "There couldn't have been that many zombies in Asheville."

"They did spill out into other areas," Amy said. "I bet they infected clear into Gatlinburg and Knoxville."

"But, why are they all coming back to," Paul spread his arms and looked about, "here?"

"They were part of Satan's twisting of reality during The Troubles. Evil. Maybe they are still driven by Satan's plan to stop us."

"Well, they seem entirely too focused on us or our community. And we completed our missions. What's left to stop?"

"Don't know." Amy snuggled up against Paul's right side as they walked.

"Ouch," Paul said. "Sorry. I'm a little sore, too. Not as bad as you, though." He gently wrapped his arm around her.

Then they saw Lucy and Sgt. Flynn carrying boxes toward sixth platoon's area.

"What'cha got there," Amy hollered.

"You won't believe what we found, Amy," Lucy said. She was practically dancing on the sidewalk. "This old sporting goods store had cases of arrows in the back!"

"Really?"

"Yep," Lucy beamed. "There wasn't much else there, but they had these. They aren't the best, but they'll work. I just went in on a hunch and look what I found! I'm taking a hundred. We'll keep them in the truck and I'll fill my quiver between fights."

"She's incorrigible," Flynn said. "All I wanted to do was have a little quiet time and talk, and she goes off foraging."

With the arrows stowed in the truck, Paul and Amy said their goodbye's. She would head south again to anchor the line at US 74.

Paul would take his platoon north toward Marion and try to hold the horde in the foothills.

SEVEN

Overrun

Amy's thoughts on holding back the horde turned negative as she rode in the truck to their next platoon area. Much as she wanted to succeed in stopping or eliminating the zombie threat, something deep inside told her it was a losing game. She prayed, but the feelings stayed. They had a lot of firepower, but it wasn't enough. The horde kept coming. And their ammunition supply was not infinite.

"I'm not sure I should offer a penny for your thoughts," Lucy said as they bounced in the back of the truck. "I know you don't want to know mine, especially regarding traveling in this truck." She rubbed her lower back and stretched.

"I'm just worrying," Amy said. "I don't usually do that. Something doesn't seem right, though."

"Yeah, I get that feeling, too," Lucy said softly. "Something is weird about these zombies and coming this way."

"You picked up on that, did you?"

"Well, you and Paul—Paul especially—were instrumental in resetting reality, and cleaning the evil out of Washington, D.C. I'm sure Satan is still trying to destroy you two."

"How much of our story do you know?"

"Well, Paul told me everything while he brought me to the community." She looked at Amy. "Some parts I had trouble believing. I mean, c'mon, you guys were just fourteen when Paul said he was called on that first mission. That's a lot to swallow."

"Oh, well ..." Amy started.

"No worries, though," Lucy waved a hand. "All that has been verified. Now I know you guys, too. Makes a lot of difference."

Lucy looked at Amy seriously.

"You do know Paul could not have done any of that without you," Lucy said quietly. "After seeing you practicing, I now understand just how much you brought to the table. Paul is so lucky."

"Thanks," Amy said. She reached out and touched Lucy's arm. "I needed that little boost."

The truck bounced hard a couple of times and stopped. Brad came around and pointed a flashlight into the back of the truck.

"Amy, you're getting out here. We're going to coordinate with third platoon at this point."

"Okay," Amy said, gathering her gear and climbing out of the truck. She looked back at Lucy. "Stay safe!"

"I will," Lucy replied.

Brad led Amy over to a trooper from the third platoon.

"This is your contact in third platoon. He is the end of their line," Brad said.

Amy shook the man's hand.

"You two will maintain visual contact until we move again, or roll up the line."

"Got it," Amy said. "I'm Amy. What's your name?"

"Teddy. Glad to meet you."

"Okay, Amy," Brad said, "it is a long way to US 74. If things get bad or we call you to roll it up, you contact Teddy. Let him know what we're doing, and get moving south. Your best route is to stay on or along is the Polkville Road here, and roll up the platoon as you go. I'll anchor the platoon at the junction of Polkville Road and US 74."

"Sounds like a plan, Brad," Amy said.

"I figure US 74 gives us the best, fastest route to the next fallback position, should we have to bug out."

Amy nodded and looked at Teddy. Teddy nodded.

"I understand your instructions," he said. "We have a similar plan for our platoon."

Brad checked his watch.

"We're getting close to dawn. As I understand from your company commander, the zombies pretty much spend the evening hours stumbling around in circles unless there is something to attract them."

"That's been our experience," Teddy said.

Brad handed Amy a small canvas bag.

"This is extra fresh magazines. Just a little insurance." He smiled at her and left.

"Thanks, Brad," Amy said to his retreating back.

"I'm set up on the roof of that building," Teddy said, pointing to the other side of Polkville Road. "My field is down Zion Church Road. If you go about a quarter mile south, there's a building you can use that has a nice open field of fire to the west."

"Thanks, Teddy," Amy said and turned south. "I'll wave when I'm set," she said over her shoulder.

"I won't be able to see that until the sun comes up. Flash a light."

That was dumb on my part, Amy thought, glad it was too dark to see the color rise in her cheeks.

#

I wonder how Paul is doing, Amy thought as she settled in an abandoned vehicle with flat tires and prepared her firing position. The vehicle was an old van, with windows all around and a sliding door on the side. She used the rifle butt to bust out the windows facing the open fields to the west. She left the slider open so she could get out quickly if necessary.

The sky started to lighten in the east.

At least I won't have the sun in my eyes. She scanned her field of fire and didn't see anything moving. She unzipped the canvas bag and set it next to her on the floor. Her belt pouches were filled with fresh magazines, and she had a full one locked in the carbine. *I wonder how often we're supposed to clean these?* She noticed dust and carbon around the carbine receiver area.

She pulled a small towel out of her pack and folded it to provide a pad for her shoulder. She took off the ice pack and tossed it aside, then placed the towel over the bruise. *That should help,* she thought as she closed up her shirt. She flashed her light in Teddy's direction.

"I'm set, no activity. Visual with third platoon, over," Amy radioed.

"Roger, out," Brad replied.

Others on the platoon net reported their status and then it was quiet again. Details in her field of fire became more evident as the sun rose and light flooded the countryside with a golden morning glow. Nothing moved. She adjusted her scope and slowly scanned the tree line about three hundred meters across the fields. Buildings to her left, and a pond with trees blocked some of the view to the southwest. But she could see past that to the wood line beyond.

The sun blazed in its rising and filled the woods across the fields in a riot of color and light. Then she saw movement. Not much, just two or three zombies shifting in the trees. Amy dialed in her scope and visually marked the two hundred meters range. And waited.

A zombie started moving across the field.

"Contact," Amy radioed.

She tracked the walker until it finally crossed the two-hundred-meter point, and she fired. It went down. Another came out of the trees a few meters south of where the first came out. She repeated the process and dropped that one. The pad on her shoulder helped. It also seemed to help that the pad caused her to hold the carbine tighter against the shoulder, so when she fired, it didn't slam against her.

Live and learn, she thought. Then she spotted three more moving out of the woods.

As she tracked and engaged more zombies, she heard others on the platoon net reporting contact. She also heard rifle fire just north of her. *Teddy must be getting busy, too,* she thought.

Amy burned through a magazine, slapped a fresh one in and charged the carbine.

The numbers coming out of the woods were sporadic. Sometimes just one. Other times, three or four. Even as the morning progressed, the number of zombies did not increase. She listened and heard just occasional rifle fire north and south.

"Brad," Amy said over the radio, "We're not seeing many zombies up here."

"Roger," Brad replied. "The company net isn't reporting anywhere near the numbers we had yesterday. It may be early, yet. Stay alert."

"Roger that," Amy said.

She watched the tree line for more, and nothing happened for a good fifteen minutes. Then, one zombie stumbled out of the woods and shambled her direction. She waited and squeezed off a round and dropped the zombie at about one hundred meters.

At what she estimated was high noon, she ate lunch. She'd only seen three more zombies since mid-morning. *Who'd have thought fighting zombies would be boring,* she thought. Her patience was at an end.

"I'm going to scout forward," she radioed on the platoon net. "Either we did a better job than we thought yesterday, or something is keeping them."

Amy swapped out her empty magazines for full ones from the bag and filled her pouches. She left the little canvas bag there, along with her pack. She got out of the van and trotted across the road and into the open field. Nothing else moved.

She kept her head swiveling and eyes scanning the woods for movement. Her goal was the part of the woods most of the zombies came from. She got to the zombie bodies, paused and looked around. Nothing moved. She continued on. Her stomach rumbled after getting an up-close look at the zombies she'd dispatched. They didn't scare her so much as creeped her out. And the smell was horrid.

At the wood line, she paused again and looked carefully for movement. Nothing. The woods were too thick to see through to the next field, so her only choice was to move through them and see what was on the other side. The woods were dead silent, except for the small noises Amy made. She crept through and finally came out on the west side where the woods continued on the left, but a field opened in front. There was another road, Barbee Road was the name she remembered from the platoon's map.

Nothing moved in the woods or in the field. She jogged across the field to Barbee Road. Houses lined the road to the south. Just to the north, it crossed Zion Church Road. She saw nothing to the south, so she moved north. The last thing she wanted to do was get in Teddy's line of sight on Zion Church Road. She didn't have to.

As she moved north, something to the northwest caught her eye, and it was coming out of the fields and woods just north of Zion Church Road. The movement reminded her of a pile of fresh earthworms she and her dad used for fishing bait when she was little. Then she realized it was the zombie horde en masse.

"Oh my," she said aloud. She turned and ran back across the field.

"Brad," she yelled on the radio. "We got zombies! Huge horde of 'em just north of Zion Church Road, and they are heading my way. I'm going back to my post, but I suspect I'll be rolling up soon."

"Roger, Amy," Brad said. "We're starting to get more contacts now, too."

Amy dodged through the woods, then across the field to the abandoned van. She slung her pack on her shoulders and zipped up the little canvas bag while she caught her breath. She heard rifle fire to the north, Teddy was seeing them now. She looked up and scanned across her field. A few zombies were breaking out of the woods.

She brought up the carbine and started firing when they were close enough. Soon, they were coming faster than she could shoot. She stuffed her empty magazines in the canvas bag and pulled out some fresh ones.

"OK," she radioed. "Amy, rolling up. I'll be running down Polkville Road. Get ready to go."

Amy left the van while pulling her bandana up to cover her lower face. *I hope Brad relayed my message on the company radio,* she thought. *Teddy needs to get out of there and head north, now.* She ran down the road spinning frequently and shooting any zombies that she saw.

"I'm joining you," a voice said on the radio. "Don't shoot me."

A trooper appeared out of some trees on the west side of the road and joined her. Amy indicated she wanted him on her right as they ran.

"Two of us now," she radioed.

Soon, they picked up a third, then a fourth. They were fighting a running engagement by this point. Amy was getting winded. As they picked up the fifth troop, they saw an abandoned factory to the west, and zombies swarming across the large parking lot surrounding it.

"We're just about there," Amy radioed.

"Got the truck fired up and ready," Brad said. "There is a lot of company. Do your best."

They passed an old mill, and crossed a railroad track, then there were zombies everywhere on their right. Amy started firing into them as she ran. She slammed fresh magazines into the carbine almost as quickly as she emptied them. The other troops with her did the same.

Then she fired her last round.

"Out of ammo," she radioed. She tossed her carbine to another trooper and pulled out the sai. The troops with her kept firing while they could. One troop, also out of ammo, started using his rifle butt on zombies who got close.

Amy buried a sai into the head of a nearby zombie, then spun and took out another. All the troops with her now used their rifle butts and struggled to get to the truck. She heard a rifle shot, and a zombie nearby went down.

That was from the truck, Amy thought. *Lucy.* She launched herself into a fresh set of moves taking out several zombies and giving the troops the space to break for the truck. Two stayed with her in her slow retreat while Lucy and others in the truck continued to pour fire into the mass of zombies. Amy felt crowded as the zombies closed around her and the two troops fighting with her.

She caught her foot on the body of a fallen zombie and fell. Panic welled up inside her, and her breathing got shallow and fast. She scrambled along the ground, doing her best to avoid contact with the horde, striking out with her sai as she could.

Shouts from the truck and a sudden flurry of gunfire slowed the zombies enough, someone was able to grab her shoulders and get her moving upright again.

Amy and the two troops finally made it to the idling truck on US 74.

The back gate hung down, and Amy tossed the canvas bag and her pack up into the back. Then, using her last reserves of energy, she turned and waded into the nearest group of zombies while the last of the troops climbed into the truck. She spun, kicked, and thrust with the sai, trying not to look into the dead eyes of those she put down.

Eight more zombies found peace before Amy ran and climbed into the truck. Lucy stood in the back of the truck firing her bow as quickly as she could, dropping a zombie with each arrow. When

Amy was up, someone banged on the back of the cab and the truck took off.

Amy sat back on the floor and gratefully accepted a towel. She used that to wipe off the zombie goo all over her. Then she tossed the towel out of the back of the truck.

#

Amy dozed on the floor as the truck rumbled down the road. She didn't care where they were going at this point. She just wanted to rest. Lucy sat next to her and they leaned on each other as they slept.

It seemed like she'd only slept a minute or two when the truck bounced and stopped. Brad came around the back.

"Everybody out. We have a little time to rest here. Get some dinner."

Amy climbed out of the truck and looked around. They were in the parking lot of a Bi-Lo shopping center. There was a small river to the east.

"Where are we?" she asked. Brad had a hard look on his face.

"Lincolnton," he said. "But I don't think we'll be here long. The company will assemble shortly."

She and Lucy found a place to eat a cold dinner.

"Those bad arrows did okay, I think," Amy said

"I didn't say they were bad arrows," Lucy said then took a drink from a water bottle. "I said they weren't as good as the ones I had."

"Oh."

"You look beat," Lucy said. Amy nodded.

"This isn't working," she said. She crossed her arms on her knees and put her forehead on her arms. "We can't stop these things. They just keep coming."

"Easy, girl," Lucy said, rubbing Amy's back. "We'll figure this out. Somehow."

Lucy looked around for a moment then back at Amy.

"I noticed you took some of your frustration out on a few of those zombies before you got in the truck."

"I was buying some time," Amy said.

"Sure."

Amy looked up at Lucy. Lucy was grinning. Amy smiled and shook her head.

"You're probably right."

EIGHT

Losses

Amy and Lucy joined the rest of the company to hear the commander speak. She looked around for Paul but couldn't see him. Then the commander cleared his throat.

"We took some losses, and we're going to have to reform our organization," he began. Amy thought her heart stopped beating. "First platoon lost three troops when they were overrun by the horde. Second and third platoons were hit hard in the center. Losses were heavy, and we will have to combine those two platoons. Fifth platoon, according to survivors, got overrun in the foothills on South Mountain Scenery Road. Paul Shannon and about half of his platoon were trapped in a large farmhouse. The rest of the platoon was able to escape under pressure and link up with the remnants of my first platoon."

Amy sat on the ground, hands covering her face. "Paul," she whispered, then she started to sob convulsively. She didn't understand it. How could Paul be lost? He was supposed to come back to her. Sobs continued to rack her body. Lucy knelt beside her and held her.

"He'll be okay," Lucy said trying to calm Amy down. "He'll be okay."

Amy shook and sobbed. *God,* she prayed, *please bring Paul back. I need him! Why Paul?* A hollow pit grew inside her, and it was dark down there. She was having trouble breathing and felt like someone had shoved a pillow over her face. Finally, she pulled hard and drew a deep breath.

Brad came over and squatted down.

"Paul's tough and smart," he said. "You know that. He's going to get out of this." He put his hand on Amy's shoulder. "I heard some chatter on the company net, but wasn't sure what they were saying until the briefing just now. Paul, his sniper, Joshua, and three of his troops got into a farmhouse and were still fighting when the rest of his platoon last saw them."

Amy perked up at that. *We have to go find him. Now!* She turned to Brad.

"We have to go rescue them," Amy said shaking. She felt she was getting some control, but it was hard, and she feared what Brad would say.

"No, I'm sorry. The horde was swarming that area. There's no way we can get back there now."

She almost lost it again, but she got a grip on herself and, with Lucy's help, stood. Lucy stayed next to her to keep her steady. The memory of Joe's death floated through her mind. The look on his face, half his torso burned away, and the smell. Amy's stomach lurched, but she fought back the nausea. "Paul's not dead," she said. "He can't be."

"No, Amy," Lucy said. "He's not. He'll come back to you."

"He's one of the best untrained fighters I've known." Sgt. Flynn appeared and put his arms around both Amy and Lucy. "He's gonna get out of this. We'll see him again soon."

Amy turned to Lucy. The knot in her stomach was gone and she saw her friend with new eyes. She saw the strong, caring friend she had in Lucy. "Oh, Lucy, please forgive me. I've been so jealous of you."

"I forgave you for that a long time ago," Lucy said. "Forgive me for my bad behavior."

"I do. It wasn't bad. I think God was trying to tell me something, and I didn't get it. Until now."

They hugged each other for a moment.

"We have work to do, now," Brad broke in. "We have a new plan. We're the only platoon still intact. First and fifth platoons are merged. Second and fourth, also. Weapons section and company HQ are still intact. Sgt. Flynn is now with us."

Brad looked at Amy and she felt his concern, but she knew he needed her to buck up. She got a grip, took a deep breath, and looked back at him.

"So, what's next?"

"We're going to head south, blow some bridges, then link back up with the company in Salisbury. We have some large rivers that will provide a barrier to the zombies. Specifically, the Catawba River and its Mountain Island Lake and Lake Wylie. If we're lucky, that'll contain them. If not, it'll delay them." Brad pulled out a map and spread it out. "Our task is to blow bridges at Brookshire Blvd that cross the lake, the bridge at highway 27 and the two rail bridges, Interstate 85, US 29/74." His finger tapped on the Interstate. "This is a big bridge, and I hope we can bring enough of it down."

"That's a lot of bridges," Lucy said.

"We have enough explosive to do it," Flynn said. "We don't have to bring the whole thing down. We just blow enough that it can't be used to cross the water. Our experience so far is that the zombies don't like water. The captain thinks if we can contain the horde at crossing points, we can sit on the other side and fire the mortars until we run out of ammo. Maybe thin the horde ranks there."

"What if they decide to swim?" Lucy looked more closely at the map.

"We'll fall back again, blow more bridges to slow them down and regroup near Raleigh."

"Do we have that much ammo, mortar rounds, explosives, all that?" Amy looked at Flynn and Brad.

"No," Flynn said, then grinned. "There are a couple vaults I need to access in Charlotte and China Grove on the way."

Brad looked at his watch. "We saddle up in an hour. We'll have two trucks, now. Put all the explosives and demolition gear in one, troops in the other."

#

Things went more quickly and more simply than Amy had imagined. From movies she'd seen, she expected to have to rig explosives all across the bridge. It turned out, all they needed to do was break one panel on the bridge. That took a few bricks of C4, duct tape, a couple of blasting caps and wire, and BOOM! Panel gone.

The Interstate 85 bridge was a more difficult problem.

"When the Interstate system was developed," Flynn explained, "then-President Eisenhower envisioned a way to move military troops and equipment across the country quickly. He'd seen how the German's did it with the Autobahn during World War II. So, the engineering specifications for the Interstate system required that bridges and overpasses could handle eighty-plus ton tanks crossing at full speed."

"What does speed have to do with it?" Lucy asked as she looked at the underside of the Interstate span.

"It's complicated. Speed, weight, vibration all play into it," Flynn said. "If the bridge can't handle the vehicle speed, the weight, the resonance of the vibration, it will collapse."

"Too bad we don't have a hundred eighty-ton tanks," Amy said.

"Believe me, I wish we did," Flynn said. "I'd use them on the horde."

"Think we can drop these panels?" Brad asked pointing to the supports under the bridge.

"Yeah," Flynn said. "I think blowing these supports will bring these panels down on this side. If I wrap enough det cord around the concrete pillars in a couple of places, that should shatter it and help do the job."

The troops all got busy under Flynn's supervision. Between duct tape, C4, detonation cord and blasting caps, the pillars supporting one end of the bridge were prepped for destruction. When it was ready, Flynn blew the charges.

The pillars turned to dust, and the panels above shifted slowly out of position by inches. Then nothing happened for a few seconds. Just when Amy was about to suggest trying something else, the panels broke loose and collapsed with ear-splitting screeching and tearing of rebar.

"We still have a rail bridge and the US 29/74 bridge," Brad said. "And we're running out of daylight."

The rail bridge went quickly, as had the two earlier. The US 29/74 bridge required that they get across to the east side first, then haul explosives and gear to the west side to set up the demolition.

Just as the day faded, Amy watched the demolition of the last bridge. She'd worried whether they had enough C4 to do this last one, but Flynn proved his expertise and got the job done.

Back at the truck, Brad told the platoon they had until later the next day to link up with the rest of the company.

"We'll find a place to set up for the night and get some rest," he said. "Tomorrow, Flynn will breach the two vaults, and we'll load up what we find. Then we'll head out to link up."

Amy didn't like setting up camp in the dark, but she was glad when she was able to curl up in a blanket and try to go to sleep. Lucy slept nearby. Someone stood watch, but no one thought anything would happen.

"Good night, Paul," Amy said and yawned. "Remember, you have to come back to me."

Amy prayed for Paul and asked God to bring him home safe. *Please, God. Please. In your son's name, Amen.*

#

The armory vault in Charlotte yielded the usual cache of ammunition, crates of mortar rounds, MREs, clothing and medical supplies. The China Grove armory, though, was different. It belonged to a Marine Reserve Unit before The Troubles.

"What does seven-point-six-two mean?" Amy asked loudly across the vault. "I have a bunch of boxes of it here."

"That's a high-powered NATO machine-gun round," Flynn said, coming over. He looked around at the weapon racks. "I don't see anything in here that would use that much seven-six-two."

In a pallet next to what Amy found were wooden boxes marked "25mm."

"And lookie what we have here!" Flynn said. "Some twenty-five-millimeter high explosive rounds."

"Is this good?" Amy asked.

"Well, if we have something that'll shoot this, yes!"

Flynn looked around some more and found a lock box. He broke it open and found a key with a tag marked "LAV-25." "Okay, I think I found what that ammo is for. Let's go look out in the yard."

Amy followed Flynn and the rest out to the equipment yard. There were a couple of trucks like the ones they used, but they didn't look serviceable sitting on their flat tires. Flynn went straight to a large shed with his wrecking bar and busted off the chain and lock. He pushed the door aside.

Inside was one of the strangest vehicles Amy had ever seen. It had eight large tires and looked like a tank with a little gun on top. There was a small open turret on the top front with one large barrel sticking out of it and a small one on the side. On top of the turret was a mount with a machine gun on it.

"Friends," Flynn said with a flourish, "may I present the LAV-25."

"That's amazing," Brad said. "And it's intact!"

"The weapons are still on it," Flynn said. "They must have been about ready to take it out when The Troubles began."

"Let's see if we can fire this baby up and move it out where we can look it over," Flynn said as he went through the rear door and into the vehicle.

Amy saw a light come on inside, then the engine cranked, caught and roared to life. Flynn's head came up out of a small hatch near the front.

"We're good! Move away now." He waved everyone out of the way.

The vehicle lurched as Flynn put it in gear, then it slowly moved out of the shed.

Flynn left the vehicle idling and came back out the rear door.

"Let's give this a once over," Flynn told Brad, and the two men crawled all over the vehicle inspecting it.

When they were done, Flynn handed Amy and Lucy a couple of grease guns he found in the shed. He showed them where to look and what to do.

"You see one of these Zerk fittings," he said pointing at the little metal knob sticking out of a joint, "you push the end of the gun on it, then squeeze the handle until grease comes out around the bearing or the joint." He demonstrated it. "Crawl under the vehicle and grease everything like this you find."

Amy and Lucy got busy. Amy found all she needed was a couple of pumps on the handle at each fitting. When they got to the other end, she saw Brad and Flynn had the other troops hauling the ammo crates and stacking them next to the LAV.

They set up a table at the rear and had the 25 millimeter chain gun out and disassembled. There were also two machine guns. One was the gun mounted in the front hull, and the other was the machine gun from the mount on top. Three troops were cleaning and checking the weapons.

"As soon as we get these reassembled and installed, we'll load the ammo," Flynn said. He pointed to the larger weapon. "This is an M242 Bushmaster 25 millimeter chain gun. It shoots those high explosive rounds we found. It does that very quickly and has an effective range of about three thousand meters." He indicated the smaller weapon. "These two are seven-six-two machine guns. They fire the other ammo we found. These are a huge improvement to our firepower. The high explosive rounds can probably take out ten or fifteen zombies at a time."

"Wish we had that the other day," Amy said. "Do you think we can go and rescue Paul with this?"

"I wish," Brad said. "It's a lot of firepower, but it just helps make what we have more effective. It's a good standoff weapon. It is no good in close quarters. The chain gun and the machine guns are long range weapons and not the kind you would use for head shots on zombies from a couple hundred meters out."

"And we blew the bridges," Lucy said.

"Can't these things swim across the water?" Amy challenged.

"Normally, yes," Flynn said joining the conversation. "The problem is, this has been sitting for a couple of years without the proper maintenance on the seals and such. If we tried to swim this vehicle, we'd just sink it. Probably kill anyone riding in it. We're lucky the engine and batteries are okay, and the tires aren't flat."

The troops got the weapons cleaned and remounted, then ammo was loaded in the weapons and storage. Additional machine gun and chain gun rounds were stored in the floor of the LAV, and the rest was loaded on one of the trucks. They siphoned fuel out of other vehicles in the yard and into the LAV and trucks.

Brad assigned three people, including Sgt. Flynn, to the LAV, and the rest of the platoon rode in the remaining truck.

NINE

Demolition

Amy dozed until the platoon linked back up with the rest of the company at Salisbury. The reports were about the same from the other two platoons. All the bridges were taken out, so the water barrier across most of North Carolina was unbroken, with the exception of Cowan's Ford Dam. First platoon had made a large barricade across the west side of the dam access. Blowing the dam was not desired and would likely have unintended consequences. Especially with a nuclear power plant next door. Blowing the bridges, Amy heard more than once, was going to make things hard on everyone later.

The LAV, or Light Armored Vehicle as someone else explained, generated a lot of excitement. The company commander, Brad and Sgt. Flynn discussed options for using it and came up with a plan.

Third platoon, as Amy learned, would return to the Catawba River and Cowan's Ford Dam with the LAV. From a position on the east side of the dam, the LAV would cover the west side access area. When the horde showed up, the LAV would open up and attempt to keep the zombies away from the barricade. If the zombies breached the barricade and began attempting to cross the dam, the LAV and third platoon would do their best to prevent zombies crossing.

Vehicles could not cross the dam, and even foot traffic was restricted to a narrow walkway. This would effectively channel the horde to a very narrow stream.

"We do not want to damage that dam or the nuclear power plant, and we want to rescue any of the people still in the area who manage those two facilities," Brad said. "We're taking those people from the dam, and we'll have the folks from the nuclear plant lock it up and come with us, too. So, take care what you shoot at over there."

#

Amy was happy that Lucy got to join her on the dam team. They had set up in the dark, but made use of some night vision devices the company had to get it done. From their position, it was about three hundred meters to the other side of the dam and a little more to the barrier.

Early dawn gave them a better view of the barrier. It turned out it was a bunch of abandoned vehicles and other debris pushed up into a mound arcing across the other end of the dam. Amy didn't think that would be a very formidable barrier at all. So far, it seemed the zombies would go over, around, or through just about anything in the way of their objective. Climbing that barrier didn't seem too much to expect of the zombies.

"But, it might slow them down," Lucy said, guessing what Amy was thinking.

"This is a good test of how effective that LAV will be," Amy said, still feeling like their efforts were hopeless. "But, I doubt very much we're going to stop them here."

"The chain gun is supposed to fire some incredible number of rounds per minute," Lucy said. "And those are high explosive rounds. I bet they do some serious damage."

"I have no doubts about that," Amy said. "But they run low on ammo, too. The question will be if we can actually reduce the horde enough before the ammo runs out."

"You're getting to be a real joy killer," Lucy said looking at her scope and adjusting it.

"My joy is in the Lord," Amy smiled up at Lucy. "Can't kill that!"

Lucy nodded, then said, "It's getting light enough, we should start seeing some zombies if they're here." She got her carbine set up into her firing position. Her bow and arrows were stacked against the wall just behind her.

"We're set," Amy radioed on the platoon net. "No contacts yet."

"Roger, out," Brad replied.

Amy used her little scope to visually mark the ranges along the top of the dam.

"I'm going to be limited to about two thirds of the way across the dam," Amy said, "and there are only a few unobstructed windows."

"There are guys up on the dam walkway who will get the brunt of the work if the zombies get more than half-way across." Lucy looked away from her scope for a moment. "You'll get your share of work, I'm sure."

"Yeah," Amy agreed. "Our main role is to decide when we can't hold 'em any longer."

"I have a contact," Lucy said, "just past the barrier. About 450 meters."

"Contact," Amy radioed. "450 meters west. Continuing to observe."

"Roger, out."

Amy looked through her scope to see if she could pick up the contact. She could see a slight blur that moved, maybe.

"I'd like to get a nice scope like yours," she said to Lucy.

"Oh, it's nice for these long looks, but I still can't shoot that far. It doesn't dial down for the one to two hundred meter shots. So, I have to work in the two to three hundred range. And, I miss a few."

"I have more contacts," Lucy said. "I have a lot more contacts. Can't count 'em."

"More contacts," Amy radioed. "Too many to count. Alert the LAV."

"Roger out," Brad said. "LAV, contacts west of dam barrier, engage."

They could hear the engine of the LAV as they moved it up a little to bring the chain gun into play. Then they opened fire. The sound of the gun roared across the river and echoed off the face of the dam. Amy watched the area as dust and smoke rose about one hundred meters beyond the barrier. The gun roared twice more, then stopped.

When the dust cleared, Amy couldn't see anything moving.

"One contact left," Lucy said.

"One contact left," Amy radioed.

Then Lucy fired.

"No contacts," she said.

Amy radioed the report.

"That was the first contact," Lucy said. "It made it to the top of the barrier."

Lucy looked through her scope. "More coming."

"More contacts," Amy radioed.

"Roger, out."

Amy heard the LAV fire again. Then two more times. Then it fired again.

"What's going on?" she asked.

"I can't tell," Lucy said. "Lots of smoke and dust and I can't see."

The LAV fired several more times. Then Lucy fired.

"Get ready, Amy," she said. "A few came across the barrier. I may not get 'em all."

"On it," Amy said.

Amy tracked across the dam with her carbine's scope. She identified one and fired. It went down. She saw another crossing, but it got obscured. She shifted a little to the right. When the zombie came into view again, she fired.

The LAV kept laying down fire on the other side of the barrier. Lucy kept firing away at the individual zombies that got over the barrier. Amy tried to get the ones Lucy missed. Then the handful of troops on the east end of the dam started firing.

I missed some, Amy thought, then she fired again. Zombie down.

#

The LAV was effective. That wasn't it. It was all numbers, Amy thought as she fired away, changed magazines, and fired some more. The LAV shredded the horde on the west side of the barricade. Hundreds still made it over the barricade and crowded into the narrow walkway across the top of the dam. They bunched up at the west entrance where Lucy reduced their numbers. Amy continued to reduce the numbers as they shambled across.

Then the rifle team on the east side cleaned up the rest.

"Need a resupply," someone from the rifle team radioed during a break in the firing.

Amy saw in her peripheral vision someone with a canvas bag run from the rear area to the east end of the dam.

At least we still have ammo, she thought, slapping in a fresh magazine.

"I'm out," Lucy said.

Amy grabbed several magazines from her canvas bag and handed them to Lucy.

Both resumed firing.

Then a strange new sound came from behind.

Whump-whump-whump.

Amy jerked around and looked at Lucy. "What was that?"

Lucy looked behind them.

"Oh, it looks like the weapons section joined us. I think that was the mortars."

Three loud explosions went off on the other side, scattering zombies like dry leaves. Mixed with the roar of the chain gun and the sporadic fire of the carbines, it was becoming a sound storm.

Whump-whump-whump, again.

"Okay, we have a little more firepower," Amy said trying to be heard above the noise.

"Hope it helps," Lucy yelled.

The LAV stopped firing, and Amy could hear shouting between the whump-whump-whump of the mortars.

"Now what's going on?"

Lucy looked back. "They're hauling ammo crates from the truck."

"That's not a good sign," Amy said. She turned back to firing at the zombies on the dam. "That's the last of the twenty-five millimeter. We've already used up all that was loaded in the LAV."

"No," Lucy said as she squeezed off a round. "That's not good."

The whump-whump-whump of the mortars was now constant, as was the resulting explosions on the west side. A few minutes later, the LAV chain gun roared back to life, laying into the zombies.

We have to be making some progress, Amy thought. She and Lucy had put down hundreds of zombies, the rifle squad must have had similar numbers, and the LAV must have accounted for thousands on the other side of the barrier. Now the mortars are adding to the total.

She took advantage of a break in the zombies crossing to look across the river. Mounds of dead zombies were scattered across the west side beyond the barrier. There was now a pile of kindling where a house once stood. Even the woods further back were decimated by the combination of mortar and LAV fire. Still the horde of zombies came through, aimed straight at the dam.

"How do they do that?" Amy asked aloud as she turned and began picking zombies off the dam again. "How do they all know where to go?"

"I want to know where they all come from," Lucy said, She fired five times in rapid succession, then grabbed for a fresh magazine. "I'm missing fewer. That was five for five."

Amy was getting used to the whump-whump-whump of the mortars. It was starting to add a rhythm to her firing and reloading. She was even starting to hum along with it.

Then it stopped.

"Uh-oh." Amy looked back to where the mortars were. The mortar men were pouring water over the tubes. "Looks like they overheated," she said turning back to her task.

The chain gun continued to roar death across the river, and clouds of smoke, fire, and dust rose above the horde. Amy heard yelling and shouts back by the mortar, then the whump-whump-whump started again.

"I'm out," Amy said reaching into the canvas bag and finding no fresh magazines. "On my last maggie."

"Me, too," Lucy said.

"Resupply, ammo," Amy radioed.

"Sorry, we're out," Brad said. "Pack it up and come back to the truck. Everyone."

That's when Amy noticed the whump-whump-whump of the mortars had stopped again, and she saw the rifle team from the east side of the dam running back to the truck.

Amy threw empty magazines into the bag and gathered up her gear.

"Let's go," Lucy said.

She looked back as she ran to the truck. The horde swarmed over the barrier and jammed into the walkway on the dam. Some fell off the dam in their rush to cross, tumbling down the front and crashing into the turbine block or the spillway water.

At the truck, Lucy got her bow out and nocked an arrow. Amy looked back, and zombies were spilling out of the east end and shambling their way.

The mortars were packed into their truck and the LAV shifted position to lay down fire with the coax and machine gun. Amy looked behind her into the truck and saw troops and civilians. The workers from the dam and nuclear plant were with them, wide-eyed and exhausted.

"Mortars ready," someone radioed on the platoon net.

"LAV ready," Sgt. Flynn reported.

"Let's roll," Brad radioed.

"Well, we left the dam and the nuke plant intact," Amy said. "For what it's worth."

TEN

Retreat

Back at Salisbury, the company commander gathered the troops again.

"First and second platoons had just a few contacts to the north and south of the main action. It seems the bulk of the horde tried to cross at the Cowan's Ford Dam. This will take them some time. From here, we'll blow bridges again, much as we did on the Catawba River. This time on the Pee Dee River. We'll blow the main crossings over the larger parts of the river south of here, but I suspect the smaller parts of the Pee Dee on the north side will be no barrier to the zombies. This effort may at least channel the horde through the Winston-Salem/Greensboro area and give us some time to prepare the Raleigh area.

"I'm sorry, but at this point, I'm running out of options." Captain Wilkerson looked sadly out at his troops. "We're low on ammo, and finding another cache may or may not help. Everything we've done so far has just slowed the horde, and we don't seem to have made a dent in its numbers. But, we're not going to give up, and we're not going to quit."

A half-hearted cheer rose from the troops.

"I think you can do better than that," the captain said.

A heartier cheer followed that, and he nodded.

"That's better. Let's get busy," he said in dismissal.

Amy turned with Lucy and headed back to the platoon area.

"We're getting closer to the community," Amy said. "Raleigh looks like a last stand for us."

"I think so," Lucy said.

"If we can't stop them, they will just drive through the community and then on to Washington, D.C." Amy looked at what was left in the ammo boxes and crates in the truck. "We need a miracle."

"I'm thinking that you and Paul are the targets," Lucy said. She kicked at the dirt with her foot. "Think about it."

Lucy took a deep breath.

"The zombies aren't spreading out in all directions. They are coming this way, to the community." She looked at Amy. "Paul's group was cut off. Our platoon seemed to get a larger number of the horde. And the dam. Why the dam? There's probably another longer way to the north or south. But, the dam? You were there."

"Are you blaming me?" Amy felt the tug of her jealousy and anger inside. She had lost Paul, and she struggled with a fear of his loss. How could Lucy blame her for the horde?

"No, Amy," Lucy said, she tried to put her hand on Amy's shoulder, but Amy pulled back. "No. But it does look like this horde is being driven to you. Maybe the community, but you seem to be the focus."

Driven, Amy thought. That brought her up short. *What would drive the horde? Is it possible there was another demon?*

"Amy," Lucy got her hand on Amy's shoulder this time, "Amy. Are you okay?"

Amy looked at Lucy. "If something is driving them, that scares me more than anything." Amy looked around and pulled Lucy to a more private side of the truck. "Paul and I faced hellhounds and a demon in Washington, D.C. But, we had a lot of help. Paul had an angel blade and a vest. I was given some kind of holy elixir. The angels came, and we had to give all that back at the end."

Tears filled Amy's eyes. She didn't want to break down and cry right now, but she was losing hope.

"Now," she sobbed, "I've lost Paul, and we don't have any of the help we had before." She struggled to regain her composure. She fought against the fear trying to dominate her. "The demon last year said there were others. We thought he was lying. What if he wasn't?"

"Amy," Lucy put her arm around her, trying to comfort. "That may not be what's going on. There may be something else. In any case, we can't lose you, too."

"I wish we had Elder Franklin here," Amy said, wiping tears away and smearing her cheeks. "But, I guess we can pray."

"Let's get saddled up," Brad said coming around the truck. "We got the civilians moved to the company HQ, so we're ready to go blow some more bridges." He looked at the two girls huddled on the side of the truck. "You okay?"

Amy straightened up. "Yeah. We're okay."

"Alright, up you go," Brad said.

She and Lucy sat together as the truck bounced out to the road and headed to their first bridge.

Father, help me be strong, and help us find a way to stop this evil, she prayed. *We are getting desperate, and I miss Paul. Please help Paul, and keep him safe.*

Amy continued to pray silently and held Lucy's hand. She knew Lucy prayed, too. *Maybe between the two of us we'll get a miracle.*

#

They started south of the Morrow Mountain State Park and blew a bridge on the road crossing Lake Tillery, and that went into the Uwharrie National Forest. Then they blew a railroad and a road bridge just below the Norwood Dam, a mirror image of the Cowan's Ford Dam. They also picked up a few civilians who worked at this dam.

As they headed south to the next dam, Amy and Lucy prayed more. Amy started to find a peace in prayer and her connection to Lucy. She scoured through her emotions and asked God for help in rooting out her jealousy. That's when she discovered she'd already dealt with her jealousy. Down deep inside there was this festering knot of guilt.

Father, what is this? She asked. *I know I'm a sinner and not perfect. I know I fail you at times. But, I also know that, by your grace and the sacrifice of your son, Jesus, I'm forgiven. What is this?*

"Look. Untie it and look inside," came the answer.

Amy was afraid to look, but she tugged at the strands of the knot and soon, she realized what it was. Guilt. Guilt over the death of Joe. It started to flood back.

Paul trotted through the borrow ditch in front of the steak house. He popped up and hit an alien with his staff, then stole his blaster stick. Good idea, she thought. When the other aliens' attention was directed to where Paul was, she quickly took two out, grabbed their blaster sticks and dove back into cover. She tossed one to Joe. Then they jumped out of cover and fired the blaster sticks at the aliens. Well, Amy did anyway. Joe hadn't figured out how they worked, yet.

"Get back, Joe," Amy yelled as she ducked back behind the jersey barriers.

Joe leaped for cover, but one of the aliens shot him before he made it.

Now she knew, she felt guilty about Joe's death. She had just tossed him the stick and assumed he could figure it out as she had. He didn't. He died. She felt responsible. She loved Joe like a brother, and she felt responsible for his death. And she'd been carrying this around with her for a few years.

But, Father, if I'm forgiven, why is this still here? She struggled with it, tried to keep it open so it wouldn't knot up again.

"I forgive you," came the answer. *"Have you forgiven yourself?"*

She spread the guilt out to look at it again. There was no way she could've known that Joe would have trouble with the stick. The strands of it tried to curl back into the knot, but she held firm. She looked at it and tried to forgive herself. It was hard, and the strands started to relax. *I don't know if I can forgive myself, but I'll try.*

This may take some time, she thought. She left the strands open, packaged up the guilt and put it away for the time being. *I'll work on this more later.*

Amy took a deep breath and opened her eyes. Lucy was looking at her.

"You were praying hard," she told Amy. "I wish I had that depth of spirit."

Amy gave Lucy's hand a little squeeze. "I'm just now finding it."

The truck bounced to a stop and they prepared to blow another bridge, this one across the Pee Dee River, just outside of the Pee Dee National Wildlife Refuge.

#

The platoon crossed the bridge on US 74, then set up to blow it. The day faded, and the sun blasted them as they looked west. Amy, Lucy, and some of the troops set up firing positions on the west end of the bridge while Flynn and the others prepared the explosives.

This was their last bridge, and Flynn told them this was also the last of the explosives.

"The rest of the company will be out of C4 by the end of the day, too," he said as he prepared to crawl over the side of the bridge. "Let's hope this does the job."

Amy brought her visor down on her helmet. She looked around. The Pee Dee River was muddy brown and flowing lazily south. She scanned to the west. There was no movement she could see. She'd be surprised to see any zombies since the blown bridges slowed and channeled them.

"I'm not sure there's enough C4," Flynn said as he climbed back up to the surface of the bridge about an hour later. His helmet light flashed around as he leveraged himself and his gear over the railing. "Let's try to blow it."

Amy helped string the wire for the switch to the east end of the bridge and watched as Flynn connected the thin strands.

"Fire in the hole. Fire in the hole. Fire in the hole," Flynn yelled, then he pushed the button. A deep thump sounded, and smoke and dust created a large cloud on the other end.

Amy watched intently until the smoke cleared. She brought her carbine up and looked through the little scope. She and the rest of the troops sighed when it became clear that the panels were dangling but not gone. A bit of concrete rail and rebar held together on each span.

"Well, theoretically, they could tiptoe across that," Flynn said. "But after seeing their capability on the dam, I think most of them that try will end up in the Pee Dee. Of course, their weight could just bring the rest of it down."

"That will have to do," Brad said. "Let's gather up our gear and load up. We're heading for Raleigh."

Amy took a shift in the cab of the truck as "co-driver" even though she didn't know how to work the manual transmission or any other controls of the large truck. She kept the driver entertained with stories and chit-chat until the first rest stop. What should have been just a couple of hours was turning into three, maybe four hours. The cause was the usual abandoned vehicles and slow speeds, especially at night. Wildlife, like deer and the small black bears, was also common on the rural highways. The LAV led the procession. Lucy managed to finagle a ride in the turret with Flynn.

At the rest stop Amy stood nearby as Flynn got with Brad.

"Can you reach the company yet?" Flynn had his map out.

"I think so," Brad said. "I heard a little company chatter on the net a while ago."

"Just wanted to run this past you," Flynn said pointing to his map. "We're here at Southern Pines. Everything to our south and east is Fort Bragg and its ranges. There's a cutoff up the road a bit, Lobelia Road, that will take us around the north side of Bragg. We might be able to find more ammo, maybe another couple of rigs with Bushmasters. I think it is worth the side trip."

"Let's see if we can contact the captain," Brad said. He got on the company net and tried to raise the commander.

"HQ, over," came a response after a few tries.

"HQ, Third platoon," Brad said. "We're making a side trip to Ft. Bragg to see what we can scavenge."

"Third platoon, HQ, roger out."

"That was easy," Flynn said.

Amy thought that just indicated how desperate things were getting.

ELEVEN

Fall Back

The side trip to Ft. Bragg was fruitful. Amy now rode as a passenger in a Humvee, and there were two more in the caravan. They'd picked up another armored vehicle with a Bushmaster mounted on top and found a large cache of ammo in a secured storage facility. Brad wasn't excited about bringing the Bradley, since it was a tracked vehicle, and he didn't think it was very reliable. However, after some discussion, Flynn had convinced Brad to bring it along.

"Look," Flynn said, "Even broke down and stationary, the Bushmaster will work. And the Bradley has a seven-six-two, as well."

"C'mon, Brad," Amy added, "take a few risks."

"I'm worried about what we can maintain and keep running," Brad said.

"All we have to do is get it to Raleigh," Amy said, not certain she really understood what might be involved. "With that, the Humvees, and the additional ammo and supplies, we should be better prepared to hold off the horde."

Flynn chuckled. "Yeah, that about sums it up."

"Well, we have just enough people to do it," Brad said. "If it breaks down, we'll have to leave it behind."

They'd filled the truck with ammo crates, and MREs filled the cargo areas of the Humvees.

Amy looked at the dates on the boxes of MREs. Then she had to do a little mental math. The date and year hadn't been something she paid a lot of attention to since The Troubles. She decided most of the boxes were good for two more years.

"Wow," she said. "These MREs last a long time."

"Well, maybe," the troop driving the Humvee said. "You get MREs with dates about a year from expiration, and you take your chances if you eat them. Fortunately, you'll know if it's safe to eat as soon as you open the packages. If it's too old, the cracker will disintegrate, the entrée will smell funny, and the peanut butter will look like concrete."

"Good to know."

"The only saving grace for MREs is the little bottle of hot sauce," he said, smiling. He pulled one out of his shirt pocket and dangled it in front of her. "Without that, most of them are pretty tough to get down. You really don't want to live on them."

"What I've had so far hasn't been too bad," she said. She'd also found the little bottle of hot sauce was nice for flavoring some of the entrées. Some entrées she didn't care for, but Lucy loved those and traded happily.

"What do you do if you get a bad MRE?"

"Bury it," the driver said. "Bury it deep." He chuckled. "Then hope there's a good one left over."

The Bradley made it into Raleigh, though Brad worried about the tracks being well-worn. "They look like they're gonna fall right off at any minute," he said.

#

Third platoon linked back up with C Company in the parking lots of a huge shopping mall at the junction of old Interstate 40 and 440 and US 1.

"Thanks to the side trip of third platoon," Captain Wilkerson addressed the company, "we now have more capability. We are going to take out bridges on the Haw River north and the Cape Fear River south and try to channel the horde along US 1. Between the mortars, the Humvees, the Bradley, and the LAV, we should be able to hold or delay the horde. We'll stage resupply caches along the highway. If we have to retreat, we'll have points set up for resupply and defense.

"As a last resort, we'll have the US 1 bridge mined. Ft. Bragg materials were a lucky find and gives us a fighting chance. Let's get to work and make life—or, unlife—miserable for the horde."

With a few chuckles and groans from the troops, Amy and Lucy turned and headed to the platoon area. The plan had third platoon as the center unit, with weapons section mortars, and would do the bulk of the work on US 1. Amy's grim countenance was hard to hide. Not that she tried.

"Yeah," Lucy said, "I think you're not feeling the love right now."

"That obvious, eh?" Amy said.

"Uh-huh."

"We'll stand off there near the river," Amy waved her arm vaguely in the direction of the Haw River. "We'll blow the heck out of thousands of zombies. But, they'll keep on coming. We'll run out of ammo. We'll back up and do the same. And, again. Until we can't stop them."

"Is there an alternative?"

"Not yet." Amy looked at Lucy. "I can't come up with a better plan right now. I just pray that the work we've done so far is slowing the horde down enough to give us the time we need. I'm just not sure what that will do to help."

"I hope we can stop them now," Lucy said.

"Me, too," Amy said but didn't look hopeful.

They worked with the rest of the platoon sorting fuel, supplies, and ammunition, distributing supplies to the vehicles, and topping off the ammunition trays for the chain guns and machine guns.

Brad came around as they were finishing and gathered the platoon together.

"The bridges have been blown," he told the platoon, "and the US 1 bridge is mined. No one saw any of the horde, yet. We'll be rolling out in about an hour. If you are done getting ready, now's a good time to get a little rest."

Amy and Lucy took advantage of a mobile shower tent the company HQ section put up.

"I didn't realize how long we've been away from a shower," Amy said as she put on fresh, clean clothes. She considered the clothes she'd removed. The camouflage shirt and pants could be washed, but the rest—no salvation for them. She stuffed the fragrant t-shirt, underwear, bra, and socks in a plastic bag. *Toss those,* she thought.

"I feel almost human again," Lucy said.

"Did we all smell that bad? Do you think the guys noticed?"

"Yeah, I think so. Flynn's been, uh, standoffish." Lucy said. "But they're getting a little ripe themselves."

"My bruise is starting to go away," Amy said. "I must be getting better at holding the carbine."

"Mine, too." Lucy pulled her shirt out to get a look at her shoulder.

Back at the platoon area, they loaded up and started down US 1 to the river. They stopped and set up ammo caches at two locations, one where the old US highway intersected and another just southwest of the town of Apex. At the river, the platoon positioned the LAV on the north side of the road and the Bradley on the south side.

The heavy woods limited the field of fire to straight down the highway, but they expected the horde to just move down it. They positioned the two Humvees with machine guns in the median. They put the third Humvee further back with the truck and the weapons section. Amy, Lucy and another trooper set up near the two forward Humvees to pick off the odd zombie that made it past the chain guns and mortars.

Brad had the weapons section fire one mortar round to mark a spot five hundred meters down the highway.

Whump. Then a few seconds later a fountain of dirt and smoke blew up in the median.

"There's your kill zone," Brad said over the platoon net. "Dial the chain guns into that range."

Amy could hear the whirring noises of the Bradley and LAV turrets and guns as they were set to the range. She looked through her scope, but the distance was too far. She would be picking off any that got past the kill zone and part way across the bridge. Lucy could reach a little further out.

This'll be challenging, Amy thought. She thought of her mom and dad, Paul's family, and others not far away in the community. The horde had to be stopped. She just didn't know of any better, more effective way to stop them.

She joined Lucy and they opened a couple of MREs. Both meals could be heated up if you added a little water. So, they sat in the median and chatted while the meals warmed. Amy spread peanut butter on her crackers and munched. Lucy dipped her crackers in cheese. They talked and laughed until the entrées were ready. Amy realized she hadn't enjoyed a friendship like this in a long time, outside of Paul and Joe.

"Thank you," Amy said between bites of the hot sauce seasoned beef stroganoff she fished out of the green bag with a plastic fork. She got out her little hot sauce bottle and sprinkled more on the stroganoff.

"For what?" Lucy's meatloaf came out in chunks on her fork, drowning in thick brown gravy.

"For being a friend. I needed this."

"Hey, you're not the only one. I needed a friend, too. And it was killing me that you didn't seem to like me much. Especially after hearing Paul praise you to the heavens."

"I'm sorry. I'm glad we got this sorted out." Amy swallowed hard, took a drink of water from a canteen and looked at Lucy. "I wish Paul were here."

"Yeah," Lucy agreed.

#

The day faded quickly, and they still had no contact. Brad had everyone take rotating breaks so they could rest or nap but still maintain observation across the river. Amy heard him report that he hadn't heard anything on the company net.

Amy knew the horde didn't seem to move much at night. It still creeped her out that they might start showing up as the light faded. But they didn't. It was full dark when Brad called over the platoon net.

"We're going to stand down for the night, with a rotating watch in the Bradley and LAV using the night vision sights," he said. "Try to rest as much as you can."

Amy and Lucy curled up on the passenger seats of the Humvees. Others slept in the crew area of the Bradley or LAV. Amy thought she'd only slept a few minutes when Brad came around and gently woke her up.

"Up and at 'em," he whispered. "We're about to have company."

It was still dark, but the eastern sky glowed with predawn. Amy learned that the watch spotted a few zombies shuffling around out beyond the kill zone.

"They're not moving this direction, just shambling around aimlessly," she heard a trooper from the LAV tell Brad.

"They must have just started to arrive as it got dark," Brad said.

"Coffee," a trooper said as he approached Amy with a large stainless steel thermos. "Where's your canteen cup?"

Amy looked around, found it, wiped it out with her shirt tail and held it out.

"Oh, please," she said. "Real coffee, not instant, right?"

"Right!" the trooper said and moved on. "I'll be around later with a sale contract on a bridge."

Oh well, instant or not, it's still coffee, she thought. Amy sipped at the hot brown liquid that also warmed her hands through the metal cup. *Nice way to wake up.* As she coaxed out the last drops, she felt more alive. She put her cup away and gathered her weapons.

Her pack and other gear were in the Humvee, so she figured out a way to use the belt loops on the back of her trousers to hold the sai. If it came to using them, she'd drop the carbine and have the sai out immediately. She loosely tied a fresh bandana around her neck. If she had to use the sai, she'd pull the bandana up over her mouth and nose to keep zombie fluids out.

The radio crackled as members of the platoon reported their status.

Amy set up in her firing position. Her effective range was just at the west bank of the river. As the day brightened, she started to see more details of the bridge, the river, and the thick woods along the banks on both sides.

"Contacts approaching the kill zone," Sgt. Flynn in the LAV radioed. "There are just a few right now. We'll engage when they get in range."

Lucy fired then. A zombie tumbled from the woods just south of the road and into the river.

"Must be a solo," she said.

Amy kept her eyes on the bridge. Nothing was crossing yet.

A minute later, the LAV fired a brief salvo. Then the Bradley fired. Then both fired short bursts. A plume of smoke and dust rose at the location of the kill zone. After a brief pause, both the Bradley and the LAV opened fire again with three short bursts.

"Now we're seeing a lot more," Flynn radioed.

The LAV and Bradley started firing more frequently.

"Can we get some mortar rounds just past the kill zone?" Flynn radioed when the LAV and Bradley stopped firing.

"On it," Brad responded. A few seconds later, Amy heard the whump-whump-whump of the mortars.

Amy couldn't see the mortar rounds hit from where she sat, but Flynn could through the chain gun's sighting system.

"Nice shooting," Flynn radioed. "That thinned the horde a little. Let's do a fire for effect at that range."

"Roger out," Brad said. Seconds later, Amy heard whump-whump-whump several times.

"Good work," Flynn radioed.

Lucy fired again. "Had a solo in the middle of the road."

Amy started to feel left out. None had made it to the bridge yet. Then something moved off to the left a little. She looked through her scope and saw four zombies shambling along through the trees on the west bank. She took a deep breath and squeezed off her first shot. A zombie fell into the river. Three more shots and three more floated away.

She looked along the bank using the scope. Two more were standing there, contemplating the water—assuming zombies could contemplate anything. She fired two more times and dropped those two zombies.

"We'll need to walk the mortars across the woods on both sides of the road," Flynn radioed. "More of them are coming, just not down the road."

"Understood," Brad replied. After a few moments the mortars spoke, and the woods on the south side of the road exploded. Amy watched as the trees shattered when a mortar landed next to them and blew chunks of wood and huge splinters across the landscape. Minutes later, the mortars shifted to the north side of the road and repeated the process.

Zombies from the woods along the south side started stumbling into the road, and the LAV and Bradley swept them away.

Flynn and Brad stopped the firing for a few minutes. The smoke and dust blew away, and Amy could more clearly see the kill zone and beyond. The area looked clear except for the piles of dead.

"Something is moving down the road," Flynn reported. "There's an overpass about two, three klicks down the road."

"Keep an eye on it." Brad said. "In the meantime, get the chain guns topped off."

Amy picked off another solo near the west bank. Lucy found a couple more along the road. Troops worked in the Bradley and LAV to fill the trays for the chain guns. The mortars were quiet. After a bit, Amy looked up from her scope and at Lucy.

"Not seeing anything along the banks," she said.

"Me either," Lucy said, then nodded toward the road. "Better get a look down the highway. Something is coming."

Amy looked. About three kilometers down the road there was an overpass, but she wasn't able to see clearly from her position. It looked like that earthworm-like mass she saw a couple days ago.

"Uh-oh," she said. "Lucy, that looks like the main body of the horde! I saw something like that near Shelby. It's huge!"

She keyed her radio. "Sgt. Flynn, can you make out that mass on the road?"

"Yes," Flynn responded. "It's the horde all right. Such a dense crowd. Moving slowly our direction."

"How long before they reach the kill zone?" Brad jumped into the conversation.

"At the rate they are moving," Flynn said, "I'd say about twenty to thirty minutes."

Brad came up to Lucy's position and used his binoculars. Amy could hear him speaking into his helmet radio.

"Range two thousand five hundred," he said. Then, "Left one hundred." And, "Fire."

Whump.

Amy watched down the road and she saw an explosion just ahead of the mass.

"Add 200," Brad said. "Fire for effect."

Whump-whump-whump.

A few seconds later the mortars hit the mass of zombies. The firing continued for five volleys.

"We killed a lot of them," Flynn radioed. Amy could see his head moving in the LAV turret as he looked through the chain gun sights. "Still a lot of them coming."

She heard Brad radio, "Drop 100, fire for effect."

Five more volleys flew out of the mortar tubes.

Flynn came down out of the LAV and joined Brad. Amy listened.

"You're going to have to 'drop 100, fire for effect' for a while," Flynn said. "But I'm not seeing an end to that mass through my sights."

Brad, still looking through his binoculars, said, "Yeah, I think so." He toggled his radio and repeated, "Drop 100, fire for effect." He brought his binoculars down and looked at Flynn as the mortars started their five volley cycle.

"We don't have an unlimited supply of mortars," Brad said. "But we can put the hurt on this mass until we can bring the chain guns to bear effectively."

"What are you thinking, then?"

"Move the mortars back to the next location and give them a chance to set up."

"Then pull us back when we start running low on ammo?" Amy asked.

"Yep." Brad glanced over at Amy. "Eavesdropper."

She felt her cheeks warm a little, but smiled. Brad smiled back at her, then went back to his binoculars. After a moment, he said, "Drop 100, fire for effect."

"We can reach that mass with the Bushmasters," Flynn said. "The effective range is three klicks or more."

"Can you start engaging at one klick?" Brad didn't stop looking through the binoculars.

"Yes."

"Let's do that. Coordinate with the Bradley and get it done."

"Will do." Flynn left.

"Drop 100, fire for effect," Brad said.

The turrets of the Bradley and LAV shifted as the chain guns were aimed further down the road.

\#

Amy and Lucy kept a watch on the banks of the river and the road. The occasional solo would appear, and they dispatched them quickly.

Brad continued to "drop 100, fire for effect" with the mortars, and Amy wondered how much longer they could do that before they ran out of ammo.

Then the Bradley and LAV fired up the chain guns, and the roar of the weapons echoed through the area. The combination of the mortars and the chain guns caused the now familiar clouds of smoke and dust where the horde was down the road.

Brad stopped adjusting fire with the mortars.

Amy swept her scope across the road. The chain guns were slamming into the horde and blasting it apart. But she could only see the front and not clearly. She hadn't fired her carbine for a while. Nothing was coming through the woods that she could see. Lucy just swept the area without firing.

Maybe we're stopping them, Amy thought. *That would be a blessing.*

"Brad," a trooper with a large radio yelled as he approached. "HQ relayed a report from first platoon. They have a huge horde moving across the New Hope Dam just north of us. They are trying but cannot contain them. We're gonna get flanked in about an hour."

"Get the mortars moving to the next position," Brad ordered. "We'll hold here for a bit, then join you. Provide HQ with our status."

The troop turned and ran back to the mortars, shouting into his radio.

"Amy," Brad said, "You and Lucy get in your Humvees and move back about two hundred meters. I'll ride in the Bradley when we back out of here. We're gonna blow this bridge."

When Amy's and Lucy's vehicles were positioned, Amy watched as the LAV moved back about fifty meters and then it resumed firing. Then the Bradley moved back and resumed firing. The horde was still moving forward, and Amy had a better view of the size of it. She looked through her scope. It was a flood of animated flesh that crept down the road. The chain guns chewed into the flood, but more just moved forward. The LAV moved back again and resumed firing. Then the Bradley moved back.

The horde inched closer and closer to the bridge. The chain guns stopped firing. The horde lurched ahead and started slowly across the bridges.

Amy could guess that Brad was going to blow the bridge spans with the horde on them. The horde was about two-thirds of the way across the two spans when they exploded into a huge bubble of water, smoke, and bodies. Gravity took over and dropped everything back into the river. Amy could see zombies tumbling as they were pushed off the west bank and into the river. Then the flood of zombies shifted and started to move north.

"Let's pull out," Brad radioed on the platoon net.

TWELVE

Raleigh

Amy's Humvee pulled up onto the interchange at New Hill. An old gas station and a huge brickyard-hardware store were on the south side of the highway. Brad, over the platoon net, directed Amy's vehicle to the crown of the overpass on the north, and Lucy's vehicle to the south side. This gave Amy and Lucy clear fields of fire into and over the woods to the north and through the buildings to the southwest.

Amy saw the mortars in front of the hardware store and next to the brickyard. She saw the truck and the other Humvee further down the highway to the east. Her driver got up into the back of the Humvee and prepared the machine gun.

"It's gonna get loud," he said. "You'll want to get your earplugs in."

Amy nodded as she got out of the vehicle and set up her firing position against the guardrail. She gently inserted the ballistic ear foams. The world around her quieted down, and her own breathing seemed amplified.

She saw Lucy setting up on her side of the overpass against the south guardrail. Her vehicle driver was preparing the machine gun on their Humvee.

Brad directed the positions of the Bradley and the LAV near the aprons of the ramps coming off the old highway that crossed underneath the interchange. The positions were elevated and gave the chain guns and machine guns on the vehicles good fields of fire.

Then there was a scramble of troops from the Bradley, the LAV and the mortars to resupply from the cache.

Amy was ready. Her pouches were full of magazines, and she had a canvas bag with fresh magazines. She had barely used a magazine full of ammo at the bridge. She looked over at Lucy, waved, then turned to scan the area north of her.

She saw a farmhouse and shop just north of her with fields and woods. More fields and woods to the northwest. Nothing was going to be a clear field, but their height on the overpass helped. Amy suspected the horde would get closer before she could see them.

So far, though, she didn't see anything moving. She did see the last pair of troops from the mortars carrying the last crate of rounds from the cache.

"We're seeing movement about two klicks out," Flynn radioed. "Northwest, zombies crossing open ground. Engaging."

The LAV chain gun fired. Amy couldn't make out the movement Flynn saw, but she saw the effects of the chain gun above the trees near the open field. Red clay dust blossomed up where the high explosive rounds hit and tore into the horde as it tried to cross the area.

Amy saw Brad with his binoculars, directing mortar fire behind where the chain guns were tearing up the terrain. Explosions bloomed beyond the open field among abandoned houses, farms, and woods. She felt a little left out since the LAV, the Bradley, and the mortars could engage so far away.

The Bradley fired, but aimed into the woods and farms south of where the LAV was firing.

Brad shifted fire of the mortars all across the area behind what Amy could see. Her driver fired the machine gun, and it made her jump. She looked at where he was aiming. He squeezed off three more rounds, and she saw some zombies go down in an open area of the woods just west of their position. It was still out of her range, but the machine gun could engage them.

She brought up her carbine and looked through the scope. There were several solos coming slowly through the woods and open fields. Amy couldn't engage them until they broke out of the woods and onto the highway near the interchange.

Both machines guns now engaged solos or small groups of zombies.

Amy scanned the areas along the ramps and highway near the interchange. Nothing moved out of the trees that she could see. She kept scanning. Then something caught her eye to the north.

Coming across the fields of the farm she noted earlier was a flood of zombies.

"Contact," Amy radioed. "Flood of zombies directly north. Eight hundred meters."

"Roger, out," Brad said. Immediately, Amy's driver shifted his fire to the flood. The LAV stopped firing, and moved back toward Amy's position. Then it fired into the flood of zombies. Mortar rounds also found them and blasted huge, temporary holes in the crowd.

But, they kept coming. Amy engaged random solos and small groups directly north.

Brad came trotting over to Amy's position.

"Wow," he said, "That's a lot." He looked through his binoculars and adjusted the mortar fire. "Fire for effect, pour it to them!"

A moment later, mortar rounds fell in increasing numbers throughout the horde.

But, they kept coming.

"We have to get out of here or we'll get cut off," Brad said. Then he ordered the mortars to leave for the next cache. "Concentrate fire on the north," Brad said over the platoon net, "but prepare to move out."

Amy could see the open fields between the farmhouse and the interchange ramp was now filled with the horde. She got up and tossed her bag into the Humvee. Her driver locked the machine gun down and got into the driver seat. He fired the vehicle up and started backing up the road as Amy climbed aboard. She fired at zombies stumbling out of the tree line across the interchange from her seat.

Both the Bradley and the LAV were moving east and firing as they went. Amy looked back where Lucy was and saw that she was in her Humvee and rolling east.

"Let's go," Brad said over the platoon net.

#

The next cache was at the interchange just before Apex. Brad positioned Amy's Humvee about two hundred meters west of the interchange. Heavy woods flanked the road on both sides from here to the interchange, but Amy and the driver on the machine gun would have good fields of fire to the north, south and west.

Amy could also bug out quickly if things got intense. She got out of the vehicle and set up next to the median guard rail. The driver set the Humvee near the shoulder on the north side and climbed up to the machine gun ring mount.

"Set," Amy reported over the platoon net. "No contacts."

Amy suspected Brad put Lucy and her Humvee over on the old US highway. It had a similar amount of woods, but more farms and homes and a railroad. Both locations would see the horde channeled along the roads due to the woods and terrain. She could see an overpass to the west. That was Friendship Road, according to the map.

How odd, Amy thought. *This is going to be anything but friendly.*

She still had a lot of full magazines. She wiped down her carbine with a rag, doing her best to clean the carbon and dust from the receiver area. The last thing she wanted was to have the gun jam because it was all dirty. The rag went into the canvas bag and she settled herself down to watching.

An hour passed, and she saw nothing. Then about thirty minutes later, the first solos started to show up. She saw them shambling along the road down near the overpass. It would still be a while, she knew, before they would be close enough to engage.

"Contact," Amy radioed. "Solos near Friendship Road overpass. Continuing to observe."

"Roger, out," Brad replied.

After about another twenty minutes, Amy squeezed off her first round. The solo dropped. She looked over at the driver, and he was looking north across the open fields and homes. She turned her attention back down the road.

There were more solos and a few small groups coming along. She let them come and started picking them off as they got close enough. The machine gun on the Humvee opened up. Amy stole a glance that direction. He was shooting at groups of zombies out among the abandoned homes northwest of her.

The numbers increased, and she started firing more steadily. She checked to her left to make sure nothing was coming from that direction. It was clear. Then she heard mortars crashing down out beyond the overpass. The smoke and dust rose among the heavy woods that direction.

Here they come, she thought as the chain gun rounds flew over her head and into the horde on the other side of the overpass. *And, that is a little unnerving.*

The machine gun was chattering away at a steady rate on her right. She checked that direction and saw that the driver was keeping the zombies back on that side.

She slapped a fresh magazine into the carbine and charged it. More zombies were stumbling her direction, even after the mortars and chain guns opened up on them beyond the overpass. But the horde kept coming, and soon it was on her side of the overpass, and she could see the squirming mass of bodies slowly moving her direction.

It has to be the shambling walk, swinging limbs, and how tightly they are packed together, their numbers, Amy thought. *From a distance it looks like someone just poured out a can of worms.*

The chain guns sent hundreds of high explosive rounds into the horde, and those rounds blasted holes into the wall of flesh. Those holes closed up quickly, and the horde kept moving inexorably toward them. Amy continued to fire and clean up the ones and twos, but it made little impact on the whole.

Her position was getting tenuous. The main body of the horde was directly to her front. Some were to the north, and the driver kept them away with the machine gun.

"Most of the hordes seems to be to my south," Lucy radioed on the platoon net. "I'm getting a few contacts, and we're able to deal with them."

"Roger," Brad replied. "We're going to concentrate the mortars and chain guns west of Amy's position."

"Thanks," Amy radioed. "We need that."

The LAV and Bradley renewed their fire on the front of the horde, and the mortars continued to pour fire into the area just past the overpass. Amy swapped in another fresh magazine and resumed picking off zombies.

Then the chain guns stopped. The mortars stopped. Amy's driver shifted his machine gun to the remaining zombies in front of her. Amy continued to pick of the odd zombie or two.

The horde was now reduced to random mounds of flesh scattered down US 1.

How did that happen? Amy questioned her sanity for a moment. Then pinched herself. *No, I'm not dreaming.*

She looked through her scope down the highway. Nothing as far as she could see. A zombie stumbled out of the woods to her right. She dropped it automatically.

"What happened?" Amy called on the radio.

"Not sure," Lucy replied.

"Either we got 'em all, or we have a breather," Brad said. "I'm checking on the company net."

After a few minutes, Brad came back on the platoon net. "We have a few groups still roaming around, but we think the horde is finished. HQ is calling us all back to the shopping center."

#

Amy rode in the Humvee leading the platoon past empty buildings and abandoned vehicles along Western Boulevard in Raleigh. Captain Wilkerson had briefed the company at the shopping center. Third platoon would return to the perimeter of the community and begin setting up positions. First and second platoons brought sightings of more and larger zombie groups, but nothing like the horde. Still they would need to be dealt with. There was time as they were slow in coming.

They still had a pretty good supply of ammo for the chain guns and the machine guns, and plenty for the carbines. Mortar rounds were dwindling, though.

She was starting to drift asleep in the warm late summer afternoon when something caught her eye. She'd seen that shape before. Sometimes it invaded her nightmares. She slapped her helmet and yelled over the platoon net.

"Stop! Stop! Take cover!" Amy pointed where she wanted the driver to stop. "Brad, come up here."

She jumped out of the vehicle and moved back to the intersection of Western and Dan Allen Drive.

"What's up, Amy?" Brad said as he trotted up.

Amy pointed off to her right, to the Wolfpack Training fields. "Aliens," she said.

THIRTEEN

Surprise

Brad's jaw dropped. Flynn, Lucy, and the rest of the platoon joined them.

"Aliens," Amy repeated. "I saw the saucers out on the practice fields as we drove by. Follow me, but stay under cover as best you can. They are extremely dangerous."

Amy started off, leading them around the buildings along Dan Allen Drive, then among the trees along the practice field. Three saucers sat in a line down the open soccer fields between the College Commons and the Jordan Hall dorms. None, Amy noticed, had their ramps down.

She crouched in the trees. Brad, Lucy, and Flynn crouched close by. Everyone's eyes were wide with surprise.

"Okay," Amy whispered. "This is weird. Every other time Paul and I encountered these guys, they blasted away everything in sight and immediately unloaded troops who did more blasting."

"Every other time?" Lucy asked.

"Yeah. The first time was when Joe was killed," Amy said, tears forming in her eyes. "The second time, Paul and I ambushed them and destroyed their ships."

The troops behind Lucy were agape at what Amy said.

"We need a little more info here," Flynn said. "Spill."

Amy quietly explained about the craft being a shuttle of sorts, and the alien troops using blaster sticks that somehow drew power from the ships. "They're about four, maybe four-and-a-half feet tall. They're kind of gray-green, but I never saw them in the daytime."

She looked at the ships a moment.

"It looks like they are facing east," she said. "See the lines for the ramps? Underneath. When they drop down, they exit toward the rear. We went inside one and looked around. But, I'm guessing they aren't looking our direction right now."

The late summer day was fading, and a glow from the ships was becoming evident.

"They are still inside," Amy said. "Like I said, these are like shuttles. There must be a mothership up in orbit."

"Oh, there're more?" Brad dragged his hand over his face.

"Very likely." Amy looked at Brad. "Paul and I took out about four shuttles worth of alien soldiers and the four shuttles. They landed troops in India and a couple of other places during The Troubles, but we don't know much beyond that. We left a couple of workers and their equipment behind not far from Choteau, Montana. That equipment was pretty big, so I bet they have something that hauls the heavy stuff."

A humming started, and one of the saucers started dropping a ramp.

"Spread out," Amy said. "Don't shoot until we get an idea what they are doing. Paul didn't think much of the alien fighting skills. Neither do I. I'd rather we get our hands on their technology now."

The ramp rested in the grass. After a minute, Amy saw aliens begin to come down the ramp. The first one was a little taller than what she'd seen before. The rest, as they emerged, were about the usual height. There were eight of them. They walked as though out for a stroll. None held weapons. The blaster sticks were hung in little holsters on their belts.

The tallest one waved toward the dorms behind where Amy crouched, and they all started walking toward the dorms.

This is not what I expected, Amy thought. *They look like they are exploring.*

She shouted, "Stop. Go no further."

The tallest alien stopped and waved to the rest to stop. They all stared around.

"Drop your weapons," Amy said. *That tall one understands me,* she thought.

The tall alien slipped his blaster stick out of its holster and dropped it on the ground. He turned to the rest and had them do the same.

"Follow my lead," Amy whispered to the rest of the platoon. She stood and stepped out of the trees with her carbine slung on her shoulder.

"Step back from your weapons," Amy said. The taller alien stepped back and waved to the rest of his group.

Amy waved to her platoon, indicating "get those sticks!" Then she approached the taller alien.

"You understand me," she said.

"Yes. I learned your American English from your broadcasts and some reading materials we acquired earlier."

"Why are you here?"

"We are lost," he said. "We are hungry. We need help."

Oh, man, Amy thought, *just what we need on top of dealing with zombies.*

The ramp on the next ship started to open. Amy stepped back, and the troops trained their weapons on that ship. The tall alien pressed a button on his collar and said a couple of words in his native language. The ramp stopped and pulled back up.

"Sorry for that," he said.

"Do you have a name?" Amy said turning back to him.

"I have chosen Harold," he said. "It is close to my name and fits your language."

"Harold," Amy said. "Okay, this is weird but, Harold, why are you lost?"

"Something ... happened," Harold said. "We don't know quite what. Suddenly, we were here." He waved his hand to the sky. "We didn't know where we were. We tried landing. Our ... boss wanted to kill everyone here and take the planet."

"Your boss?" Brad came up and stood next to Amy, his carbine slung over his shoulder. He looked back at the rest of the troops. "Take a knee, people."

"Yes, we had a boss that ..." Harold waved his hands and looked like he was struggling with a concept. "We no longer have that boss. We lost some shuttles and some of our people, then something happened again."

Amy knew what that something was.

"Well, that 'something' is difficult to explain, but I know what happened," Amy said. "So, why are you back?"

"We don't know where we are," Harold said. "And we had a ... fight on our big ship. It is now broken. We can't go where we were going, and we can't go back home."

"It's been more than two years since The Troubles," Brad said. "You've just been sitting in orbit all this time?"

"Orbit, yes," Harold nodded. "Our big ship stayed there. We had a big fight because the old boss was ... uh, wrong? Bad? We saw what happened on this planet. Lots of death and destruction. We tried to fix our big ship, but we couldn't. We ran out of food."

"So," Amy started, "you came back down here."

"Yes, if we stay in the big ship, we will all die."

"We need Elder Franklin and James," Brad said. He found his trooper with the company radio and called out to have them brought to the fields. "The captain will bring them here," he said when he was done. He looked at Amy. "This is going to blow everyone away. We should get the rest of the folks out of the other ships. Maybe get them fed. We have a lot of MREs in the vehicles."

"Can we bring the rest of your people out of the ships, Harold?" Amy asked. "We want to collect all the blaster sticks for now, though."

Harold nodded and touched the button on his collar. After a few crisp words, the ramps on the other two saucers lowered. Brad directed the troops to gather the blaster sticks as the rest of the aliens came down the ramps.

Two Humvees rolled up and troops started preparing MREs to feed the aliens. Amy watched as the troops stared in wonder at the smaller gray people.

"I hope you can eat what we eat," Amy told Harold.

"I think we can," he said. "We've been eating rations from the big ship for a while. This will be very welcome, I think."

"These are field rations, Harold. Our fresh food is much better, but this will get your people fed for now." Brad said.

#

Elder Franklin and James Carson arrived with Captain Wilkerson in a Humvee as daylight faded. The aliens were still eating by camp lights the troops had placed around the field. Amy thought the aliens were enjoying the MREs, though they didn't seem to like the ones with pork or bacon. *How could they not like bacon?* she thought. Brad led the elder, Carson, and the captain around to meet some of the aliens and see the shuttles.

"Well, this is good," Amy said as she sat with Harold. "We'll know how to help you in the future. To be honest, this is the most beef I've eaten in the last couple of years, from the MREs. At home, we have more vegetables, chicken, and eggs."

"Beef?" Harold looked up at her from his package of stroganoff. "What is beef?"

"That is the brown stuff you are eating with the noodles."

Harold nodded. "It is good. I like the noodles."

Amy thought his large eyes, delicate nose, and almost lipless mouth were so stereotypical of the usual depiction of space aliens. However, as she spoke with Harold, she saw feelings displayed in his expressions. Harold had a small smile as he ate. Her heart almost broke as she realized these were the same aliens she, Paul, and Joe fought. And she carried guilt over Joe, and killing the aliens, and her anger over Joe's loss. She dug down into herself again. There was that knot of guilt and anger, and it was open. She now knew what was all bound up there. She pulled at the threads of the anger, hate, and guilt. She looked at them and recognized them for what they were. Then she let them go. Soon, the knot was gone.

Jesus, please forgive me for all this anger, hate, and guilt, Amy prayed. *I see now that I need to let it go and forgive myself. In your name I ask this, Amen.*

When Harold look up at Amy again, she had tears running down her cheeks.

"What is wrong?"

"Nothing is wrong, Harold," Amy said. "I just realized something about myself."

"You are self-realizing?"

"Well, self-understanding, yes," she said. "I think I understand myself a little better. I hope that understanding helps you and your people."

Harold looked at Amy for a moment, then nodded. "I think I see. There is a lot of story about you I want to know."

Elder Franklin came around just then.

"Amy, I heard about Paul," the elder said.

Amy stood and was going to say something, but just fell into the elder's arms sobbing.

"It's going to be okay," the elder said comforting her as best he could. "We'll find Paul. I have a feeling he is just fine."

Amy was totally embarrassed. She was crying in front of the alien, then collapsed sobbing on Elder Franklin. *Pull yourself together, girl,* she told herself. She took a deep breath and pulled away from the elder.

"I'm sorry," she said wiping her face with her bandana. "It just hit me when I saw you."

"I'm here for you, Amy," Elder Franklin said. "So, who is this?" He indicated Harold.

"This is Harold," Amy said straightening herself. "Harold, this is Elder Franklin. He is my friend and spiritual leader."

"I'm very pleased to meet you, Harold," the elder held out his right hand to the alien. Harold looked at the hand a moment, then reached out his. Elder Franklin gently gripped the alien's hand and shook it. "Very pleased, indeed."

"I am pleased to meet you, Elder Franklin," Harold said. He looked at his hand after the elder released it. Then he looked at the elder and smiled his thin smile. "That was also pleasant. The hand hold."

"We call it shaking hands," Elder Franklin said. "It is a greeting custom we have."

The elder sat down with Amy and Harold and asked Amy for a briefing on what was going on with the aliens.

She told him what Harold had shared and connected the timelines for the alien's arrival and The Troubles.

"So, now, we have them as refugees from a dying starship," Amy said. "Harold is pretty good with our English."

"I'm not the only one, but I was chosen to lead this first exploration," Harold said. "I cannot believe how fortunate we are."

"How many are still on your starship?" the elder asked.

Harold thought a moment. "There are about five hundred more on the big ship. We have three more shuttles and some equipment movers. We will need to bring everyone down soon. Our big ship will die soon."

"Well, we can't ask for a better location," the elder said. He pointed to the dorms across the fields. "I don't know if we have running water or working sanitary facilities, but there is some ready housing. A landing field right here. I don't think this part of town has power, though."

"We have power," Harold said, pointing to the shuttles. "We can provide that."

"Yeah," Amy said. "The shuttles are a source of a broadcast power. They provide power for the blaster sticks, as well as weapons on the shuttles. I suspect they have ways to harness that for lights and other devices."

"Yes, we can show you," Harold said, his eyes lit up.

"Can we have your boss come down, next?" Amy asked. "The elder and others can work with him and get everything set up so your people can all come down."

"Yes," Harold said. "The boss is ... my ... wife." He smiled and touched the button on his collar once more, then said a few words. "She will be down shortly."

#

People from the community came out to help get the dorms prepared for new residents, trying to get the plumbing working and fix electrical problems. Amy watched some of the preparations, but was called away by Brad.

"We have work to do," Brad said when the platoon was gathered. "There are two large groups of zombies coming upon Raleigh. One is coming down US 1, the other is coming along Interstate 40. We have to split our assets. The Bradley and one of the Humvees are going to first platoon. We keep the LAV. First platoon gets the mortars, but they are almost out of ammo, so it doesn't make that much difference. We have Amy and Lucy."

"Thanks," Amy said grinning.

"Our reports came from scouts from first and second platoons who tried to stay close enough to the groups to track where they were going. We don't know if there is anything behind these groups. We're going to set up on US 1 at the Ten Ten Road interchange. We have chain gun ammo to split and then load up. We roll in an hour."

Amy turned to find her Humvee. Harold was standing behind her.

"You go to fight," he said. "We saw your fight. You are not doing well. Your enemy is big."

Amy's eyes went wide.

"Yeah," she said. "Yeah, our fight is not going well."

"Can we help?"

"Well, it isn't your fight," Amy said.

"But, this is now our home," Harold said. "So, it is now our fight."

Amy looked at Harold. The aliens weren't the best soldiers, she knew. She and Paul, well, that's another story. But, she couldn't just hand the aliens their blaster sticks and send them after zombies. That would be cruel. Already, the shuttles were making trips up and back from the big ship bringing the rest of their people down.

"Oh, Harold, you shouldn't have to join this fight just as you are arriving," Amy said.

"We have to come here, or we die." Harold's eyes misted. "If you lose this fight, we will probably die. We must help you."

He was right. Amy knew it. Now, how would this work? She called Brad over and explained what Harold volunteered.

"What we need most," Amy said, "is good information on what is coming. Can we use one of your shuttles to see where the enemy is and how big they are?"

"Oh, yes," Harold said, brightening. "We already know some, but we can show you. My wife said I can use two shuttles. The rest will bring my people."

"Can Amy ride with you in one of the shuttles?" Brad asked. Harold smiled and nodded. "Okay. I'd like to send Sgt. Flynn in the other one. Can we do that?"

"Yes, we can do that."

"Flynn," Brad called out. "Your dreams are coming true."

"If the saucers are going to be within about a thousand meters of the troops on the ground, we should distribute the blaster sticks around to the troops, too," Amy said. "I've seen what they can do, and they may be better than the carbines."

Brad's eyebrows tried to crawl over to the back of his head.

"I'm not kidding," Amy said. "Wait 'till you see the firepower of these shuttles."

"Let's do this," Brad said.

Amy walked up the ramp of the first saucer with Harold. It was the same as she'd seen before. There were harnesses around the wall for passengers to strap in. She knew the screen over the control console displayed what was in front of the saucer, but Paul messed with that more than she had.

Harold pushed a button on the console and the ramp lifted into the bottom of the saucer.

"Do I need to get strapped in?"

"No," Harold said. "That is only necessary for ... in and out of orbit. You can stand here next to me."

Amy watched him work the controls. They consisted of a hemisphere that he moved one hand across and a lever that he pulled back or pushed forward. There was a large button on the right, and she remembered Paul had pushed that to fire the weapon.

Harold pulled the lever back, and she felt the saucer lift. She heard a thud which she hoped meant the landing struts pulled in. Then Harold's left hand started to move across the hemisphere, and the saucer banked and turned. She saw the landscape change on the screen as the saucer turned, and they headed southwest to US 1.

At this rate, they would be at the Ten Ten Road junction long before the rest of the platoon. Howard reached up to the screen and touched it, dragging his finger up about an inch. The screen looked almost like the night vision sights they'd used, but much clearer and brighter. She could see details as if in clear daylight.

In only minutes, they were at Ten Ten Road.

"Brad, Amy," she called over her platoon radio. "We're at Ten Ten. No contacts. We'll scan around the area."

"Roger," Brad replied. "We're about ten minutes out."

"Roger, out."

She looked at Harold.

"Can we look around the area some?"

"Yes!" Harold began to move the saucer to the north.

Amy watched on the screen. Twisty roads ran through neighborhoods, much like the one she and Paul lived in. The occasional swimming pool, all green from algae. Shopping centers and open fields of red clay. They turned south, and she saw about the same thing. Nothing moved.

Harold circled the saucer back to the Ten Ten Road junction.

"So far, it's clear," Amy said. Harold nodded.

"Brad," Amy radioed, "Ten Ten is clear. We're going to move along US 1 a little to see where the horde is."

"Roger, out," Brad replied.

Amy nodded at Harold and he moved the saucer along over US 1.

She recognized some of the terrain they had moved through earlier in the day, mostly wooded with some farmland. Then she saw the horde. Well, a small horde, or large group—her perspective was out of whack by being at altitude. It moved slowly up US 1 across the interchange they had set up in that morning.

"Contact, over," she radioed. "Large group moving across the state highway interchange." She did a quick mental calculation. "About thirty minutes from Ten Ten."

Harold studied the screen for a few minutes.

"Those are ... bad. They are not alive. They are sick," he said. "But, they move. How is that?"

"They are called zombies," Amy said. "Some disease or parasite or something takes a dead person, or kills the person and re-animates the body."

"That is ... sick." Harold shook his head. "That is ... bad. I think your word for that is 'evil'?"

"Yes, evil."

"But, they only come this way?"

Amy felt a twinge in her gut.

"Yeah," she said. "We don't know why."

"We must find out why." Harold raised his hand with a finger pointing up. "We must find out why."

"We have about twenty minutes, Harold," Amy said. "Can we go further down the highway and see if there is anything more back there?"

"Yes, we can," Harold said and started moving the saucer. "But, I already know there is more. We could see that from ..." he pointed up, "up there."

"You could?" A realization of what Harold was saying earlier began to dawn on her.

"Yes. Big enemy."

Oh, my, Amy thought. *Even with the help of the aliens, could they beat this?* She had to see first, though.

#

Harold flew the saucer down US 1 until Amy had him stop just above the brickyard. She looked at the blown bridge across the Haw River. She didn't see any movement in that area.

"Can we go north a little?" she asked. "There's a dam just up there."

The saucer glided over the countryside, and the screen brought the dam into view.

"There is the big enemy," Harold said. "Big enemy."

Amy's jaw dropped. A huge horde was jammed up against the west side of the B. Everett Jordan earth fill dam, streaming across the top, and spilling out on the east side. Other than crossing the dam, the horde wasn't making a lot of progress east. Amy guessed they were just waiting for morning.

"It looks like about a third is across the dam," she said.

"I think so," Harold agreed.

"Brad, Amy," she radioed. "Major contact. Huge horde. At the earth fill dam."

"Roger," Brad said. "So, this group isn't the last of them."

"No."

"Roger, out."

She looked at Harold. "Can we shoot this?"

"Yes." Harold swung the saucer across the body of the horde, came lower, aimed obliquely, and pressed the large button. A beam shot out of the saucer and into the horde. Everything it touched turned to flame and ash as it swept across. Harold released the button.

When the screen readjusted from the brightness of the beam, Amy saw the results. A huge swath was cut across the horde on the east side of the dam. It was rapidly filling back in with more zombies, but it proved to Amy that the saucer's weapon was viable.

"Excellent," Amy said. "Thank you, Harold. Let's go join the platoon at Ten Ten."

Amy radioed they were bringing the saucer back to Ten Ten Road.

They passed over the group coming down US 1 toward Ten Ten Road on the way.

"This is a hard thing," Harold said. "I don't like to kill. But, those ... they do not live. They are already dead. My heart is confused."

"I understand, Harold," Amy said. "I don't like it, either."

At Ten Ten Road, Harold turned the saucer to face the southwest again. The zombies were just starting to appear around the long bend of the road. Amy could hear the LAV and the machine gun open up on the first ranks of zombies.

"The ... blaster sticks, as you call them," Harold said. "They cannot shoot so far. This can." He patted the console. "But this hurts more."

"Yeah," Amy said, watching the zombies continue to advance in spite of the heavy fire from the platoon.

The group was channeled by the woods thick against the side of the road, so this stretched them out. Smaller groups and solos spilled out on the frontage roads on either side. Amy was amazed at how much advantage the saucer gave her in seeing the whole field.

"I have an idea," she said. She couldn't help but give Harold a little shoulder hug.

"Brad, Amy," she radioed. "Let's try something. Get out the sticks. There is a little button on one end. Point the other end at the enemy and push the button, that's how they work. Get the platoon moving down the lanes of the road. We'll blast the main body from above, you can clean up as we go along on the sides."

"Okay," Brad replied. "That'll save ammo for the really big group."

"Yeah," Amy said, then turned to Harold. "Can we just slowly move forward and shoot along the road?"

"Oh, yes," Harold said, and he started moving the saucer and shooting the blaster.

They swept the main body of the zombies off the road as they moved. The platoon in their vehicles below blasted away solos and small groups along the sides and frontage roads. The work took just minutes, and when the zombies were gone, Harold landed the saucer in the middle of the road ahead of the platoon.

"That went well," Brad said as Amy came down the ramp. "You were right, that saucer has some serious potential. We should relay this tactic to the first platoon."

"That is done," Harold said, indicating the button on his collar. He was silent for a moment, then tapped the button again and smiled. "They have done the same and are victorious."

"Fantastic," Brad said.

"But, you still have a big, big, enemy," Harold said, waving his hand in a generally west direction.

FOURTEEN

Merger

Amy crept around the corner of the house. She heard movement, steps from inside. All around her lay burned up zombies. The stick felt warm from use and hummed in her hands. She kept her finger close to the little firing button.

The front door crashed open and a figure stumbled out. Amy drew the stick up to fire as the figure turned to her. Its head tilted at a strange angle with the side of the neck bloody and torn, its skin sallow and its eyes dark sunken pits. She almost pressed the firing button when she realized it was Paul.

"Paul," she said. The figure just shuffled toward her. No recognition in the staring eyes or face. She froze. "Paul," she cried.

Brad appeared on her left and fired a blaster stick and burned Paul to a pile of ashes.

"No!" Amy shouted. "No!"

"Amy," someone said. "Amy. You are dreaming."

She felt a gentle touch and shake of her shoulder. Her hand was tangled in a blanket and she struggled to get it free to brush her hair from her face.

"Gently, Amy," the voice said. "Gently."

Her hand came free and she pushed herself in to a sitting position and brushed her hair back with her hands. Harold crouched nearby. She looked around at the interior of the saucer. She had been curled up on the floor with a blanket and pillow. *I don't even remember going to sleep,* she thought.

She pulled out a bandana and wiped at her eyes and face.

"How long have I been asleep?"

"A few of your hours, I think," Harold said. "You were very tired. It will become day soon. I think the enemy will arrive as well."

"Let's go see if anyone made coffee," Amy said. She got up and stretched, then folded the blanket and put it on the pillow. Her hand shook a little as she smoothed the folded blanket. *That dream reflected my greatest fear right now,* she thought. She followed Harold down the ramp.

The aroma of coffee floated in the pre-dawn air and she followed it to the back of the truck. An enterprising trooper had a pot boiling and made coffee from the freeze-dried packs from the MREs.

"Make mine extra strong," she said. "And add a pack of cocoa." It would have to do. Nothing beat good fresh brewed coffee. The freeze-dried was never close to the flavor or experience of brewed, in her mind. But the cocoa helped make it palatable.

Amy looked over the selection of meals and picked a couple of good breakfast MREs.

"Let's have breakfast," she said to Harold, and they set about heating and eating the meals.

As they finished, Brad came over.

"Can we get you to take the saucer up and scout ahead?" he asked Harold.

"Yes," Harold said wiping his mouth with a napkin. "The enemy is moving now." He pointed to his collar. "I have a report from the big ship. Also, the last of our people are leaving it now."

"Good to know," Brad said. "So, some of the information you had came from observation from the big ship?"

"Yes," he nodded. "But now no one remains, and we will go back up to take out ... materials."

Amy followed Harold back into the saucer. They lifted off and flew down the highway. Daylight broke slowly over the land, and Harold adjusted the screen in front of the control console. As they approached New Hill, Amy could see the leading edge of the horde moving toward the highway.

"Brad, Amy," she radioed, "contacts. The horde is moving near New Hill. They are about forty minutes from your position. We're going to see how big the horde is."

"Roger, out," Brad said.

"Let's go toward the dam," Amy said pointing.

"Yes," Harold agreed.

In the daylight, they could see the vast numbers of zombies spreading across the villages, farms, and woods. *You can't drop a rock down into that without hitting a zombie,* Amy thought. The horde overran everything from New Hill almost all the way back to the dam, and from the shores of Jordan Lake in the north to Harris Lake in the south.

"I think we're going to need the other saucer here," Amy said.

Harold nodded agreement, touched the button on his collar and spoke a few words.

"They will be here soon."

"In the meantime, let's soften this up a little," Amy said. She pointed to an area west of New Hill. "Let's come in low here and sweep that area."

Harold maneuvered the saucer into a low approach and then swept the area with the beam weapon until only wisps of smoke rose from the ground. Zombies slowly filled the area, but Amy thought they made a dent in the numbers. A very small dent.

She pointed out another area a little further west, and Harold brought the saucer around and repeated the process. Amy couldn't guess the numbers in the horde, but she estimated the two sweeps they just made took out a couple of thousand undead.

The other saucer arrived, and Harold tapped his collar button and had a brief conversation.

"They are going to the other side of the horde and will do what we've done," Harold told her. "We should try to make the enemy smaller."

"Agreed," Amy said, and pointed to another area a little further north.

After a few more sweeps, Amy thought they should return to the platoon and prepare to meet the horde head on.

"We're coming back," she radioed. "The other saucer joined us."

"Roger," Brad said. "I heard from Flynn. Good work."

"See you soon."

#

By the time the saucers found the platoon, Brad moved them to the state highway interchange.

"I think we slowed the horde down a little," Amy said to Brad when he met her at the bottom of the ramp. "It looks like they're still about fifteen minutes away. But they are stretched across the country and not limited to the highway."

"I figured that," Brad said. "That's why I moved here. It gives us some fallback room. We can hit 'em, let 'em coalesce, then hit 'em again."

"Good plan."

"Not so much plan as desperate hope."

In spite of the dire nature of their situation, Amy laughed. It felt good. Brad even smiled.

"Harold said the two saucers would move above and sweep the road and out to the sides," Amy said. "We're going to take out trees and anything else there, so that will remove a lot of the nearby cover. That should open things up for the LAV and the troops."

"Sounds good."

"Up we go," Amy said. She waved at Brad and went back up the ramp.

Harold raised the ramp and lifted off. He touched the little button on his collar and had a brief conversation. Then he started moving the saucer slowly forward. He swept the blaster from the center of US 1 to about one hundred meters south. Everything in the path burned to ashes; houses, buildings, trees, and the leading edge of the zombies. Amy could see a similar action by the other saucer on the far right of the screen.

They hadn't moved far when Amy heard the chain gun open up below and behind them. Evidently, the zombies were collapsing into the empty area.

It wasn't long, and most of what the blaster was burning involved the thick mass of the undead.

I hope this takes the pressure off the platoon, Amy thought.

Harold finally looked at Amy. Tears streaming down his face surprised her.

"Are you okay, Harold?"

"It is painful," he said. "I know they are not alive, but it is still painful."

She put her hand on his shoulder. "I understand," she said. "This makes me feel awful, too."

"The alternative," Harold said, "is becoming one of them. I have to remember that this is a mercy we do."

"I think we need to go back to the platoon now," Amy said. Harold nodded and touched his collar button.

After coordinating with the other saucer, he banked around and moved back to the platoon's position.

They repeated the process several times, but by the middle of the morning they'd only reduced the horde in front of them by about a third. It continued to move into the areas burned clear by the saucers, and the troops and the LAV continued to decimate the leading edge of the horde. But they were losing ground.

Brad radioed that the platoon would move back to the interchange at the Walmart shopping center when the saucers began their next sweep. Amy acknowledged the move, then noticed a small red light blinking on the control console.

"What's that?" she asked.

Harold glanced at it. "Our blaster is getting overheated. We will need to ... rest it for a while."

"How soon?"

"Soon."

"Would it be possible to bring a few more shuttles from the landing site?" Amy asked.

"Yes," Harold said. "I will ask."

After a short conversation, Harold looked at Amy. "They are sending two more. That will give us a rest and still hold the enemy."

"Thanks," Amy said. Harold was looking a little tired. He had been concentrating hard on the sweeps for a few hours now. He was probably ready for a rest and something to eat. "Thank you so much."

Harold tapped his collar button again and had a lengthier conversation. When it was done, he smiled and banked the saucer around and headed to the platoon's new location. The little red light was still blinking, but more slowly. It was a short trip, and soon they were landing in an empty area of the Walmart parking lot.

"I need rest, too," Harold said after he lowered the ramp. He got the blanket and curled up on the floor of the saucer with his head on the pillow.

"Rest well, friend," Amy said and walked down the ramp.

The other saucer had landed nearby with Flynn coming down the ramp. Evidently, his pilot was resting, too. And Amy saw the platoon's truck parked not far away. She strolled over to it.

Flynn reached the truck at the same time. He gave Amy an odd look. She wasn't sure what he was about to say, but hoped it was something positive.

"You surprise me, Amy," Sgt. Flynn said. "I've seen you on the ground fighting, and you are a natural. Like Paul. As I understand you two were quite the team."

Amy nodded, struggling to hold in her grief.

"My pilot said that the aliens are learning a lot from us—from you. It seems they had never thought to use the saucers this way until you and Harold did it."

"I just had an idea," she said, then she remembered how the saucer in Buffalo, Wyoming came through shooting the blaster ray at random targets. She grabbed two MREs out of the back of the truck and tossed one to Flynn. "I've seen what they can do and thought this would work. I didn't know about the overheating."

"My pilot—he calls himself Jeremiah—said they knew about the overheating, but hadn't redlined the blasters before." He looked at the MRE package and frowned. "Oh, my favorite. Hot dogs. Yum."

"Is Jeremiah resting now?"

"Yeah, he just about collapsed after he lowered the ramp," Flynn said as he got the meal heating. "I think our new friends aren't acclimated to our planet yet. Maybe they aren't used to our gravity, either. Their build—I think they are from a planet with a little less gravity."

Amy nodded as she opened her warmed meatloaf package, letting a little steam out. "When we get time, it will be great to just spend time getting to know them and learn about where they came from."

"From what Jeremiah said, they are going to scrap their ship and bring it all down eventually." Flynn sprinkled hot sauce and squeezed ketchup into the pouch of hot dogs. "Well, now it won't taste so obviously of boiled hot dogs."

"I have some of the good crackers," Amy said, "want some?"

"No," he said. "I could use more Tabasco. Got any?"

"Yeah."

#

Harold told Amy that the saucer needed about another hour to cool down, so he sat at the truck and ate. Amy hiked over to the platoon position on the interchange to see the action from the ground.

When she walked up, she was surprised to see fifteen aliens working with the human troops in rifle squads, or blaster stick squads.

"The two new saucers brought them out," Brad said when he saw Amy observing. "They learn quickly and work with our people well. The language barrier is a little sticky, but we manage. A few know some English—enough to understand what we need to do—and those slick little collar radios they have help get things translated."

"Looks like we'll have some things to learn from them when we get this job finished," she said.

"Our machine guns and the chain gun cause them some stress," Brad said. "The noise and concussion when they fire. They are managing, though."

Amy watched the two Humvees, loaded with a blaster squad each, swing down each side of the road mowing down zombies as they tried to coalesce into the vacant area left by the saucers.

"They keep coming," Amy said. "They just keep coming."

The saucers left the woods west of the interchange completely cleared and smoking about three or four hundred meters across. The horde still moved their direction and collapsed into the vacant landscape, but it seemed they were much slower now than earlier in the day.

An alien approached. This one was definitely female Amy thought. Her form and features different from what she saw with Harold.

"This is Ruth," Brad said. "Harold's wife."

Amy immediately reached out her hand, "I'm so glad to meet you!"

Ruth smiled and took Amy's hand.

"I am very pleased to meet you. Harold is resting, I assume," she said. "He ... described you to me."

"It turns out the materials they had for learning English were limited," Brad said. "Ruth said one of the books they had to read was the Holy Bible. Turns out that is where a lot of them are picking their names."

"Ruth is a good name," Amy said. "A good choice."

Ruth nodded and smiled.

"Harold said you are the boss," Amy said. "Like the ship's captain?"

"Captain?" Ruth looked puzzled for a moment, then nodded. "Yes, I think that might be a good word. I lead our people. We have many difficulties. But we are pleased that we found you and can help. Your people have been very good, very ... generous."

The other two saucers came floating back and headed to the parking lot.

"I have to run, sorry," Amy said. "It is our turn."

She ran back to the saucer and up the ramp just as Harold was getting it ready. He raised the ramp and lifted off right away, pulling in the landing gear. Amy looked over the console. The little light that was blinking red before was now just a steady white glow.

"I met your wife," Amy said. "She was very nice."

"I know," Harold said as he brought the saucer around to start a sweep. "She told me. She said you were nice, too."

"Your little communicators are pretty cool," Amy said.

"No, they are just fine. Not too cold." Harold was preoccupied with the controls at the moment.

"I meant that they are very useful," she corrected. "I suspect you didn't get slang in your study of our language."

"Oh, I see. No, we did not. We will have to explore that in the future."

After two passes, Amy finally decided to ask Harold if she could try flying the saucer. She'd observed him enough that she thought she had a handle on the elevation and speed controls, and the blaster controls were pretty straightforward.

"So, could I try flying this?" Amy asked as they maneuvered back to the platoon position to start another sweep. "I've been observing quite a while now. I think I could do it."

"It isn't difficult," Harold said. "I think you can do it."

He swung the saucer back around and they were set for another sweep. Harold stepped to the side and let Amy at the controls.

God, please help me and don't let me crash this saucer, Amy prayed silently.

"Push the speed lever a little forward," Harold said. "Good. Now sweep the blaster."

She moved her hand across the hemisphere to direct the blaster and held down the firing button with the other hand.

As they came to the end of the sweep, Amy let the firing button go and pressed the speed lever slightly left. The saucer banked a turn, and she headed it back to the platoon position.

"I can see why this is hard for a long period," she said. "You must concentrate on directing the fire and hold down the button. Too bad you don't have a fire-lock for the button. That would help."

"A fire-lock?"

"Something that locks the firing button down for this kind of thing."

"That would be a good idea," Harold said. "But I hope we never have to do this kind of thing ever again."

Amy smiled. "Agreed."

Harold supervised Amy's operation of the saucer until the little light on the console turned red and started blinking.

"Time for us to cool down," Harold said. Amy swung the saucer back and headed to the parking lot.

FIFTEEN

Patrons

Amy hadn't been keeping track of the size of the horde. When she rejoined the platoon on the interchange, Brad told her some good news.

"We'll be done before dark," he said.

Surprised, Amy looked out across the smoking ruins of the North Carolina countryside. The other two saucers were starting what looked like the last sweep. The rest of the day would be taken up with cleaning up the solos and small groups scattered throughout the surrounding woods.

"So, Amy," Brad said. "Take a break, get some dinner. Relax. Ruth has gone down to visit with Harold."

Amy nodded and started to turn to go.

"By the way," Brad's tone stopped her. "I heard you operated the saucer most of this last turn."

She turned back to Brad. "Uh, yeah. That's okay, isn't it?"

Brad smiled. "Sure, I'm glad we're cross-training. I didn't know until Harold told Ruth. He said you were a natural."

Amy smiled and shook her head as she turned and trotted back to the truck. She found an MRE and set about warming it. Harold and Ruth came up as she worked in the back of the truck.

"We have eaten," Harold said when Amy offered them some MRE packages. "Thank you."

"We just wanted to visit with you," Ruth said.

They gathered around a small table, and Amy ate while Ruth grilled Amy about the fire-lock idea she had while flying the saucer.

"I just thought it would be a good idea," Amy said. "If Paul were here, he's the one I think could tell you how to make it. He's pretty smart about things like that."

"I would like to meet Paul," Ruth said.

Tears welled up in Amy's eyes just then, and Ruth looked shocked. Amy grabbed a napkin and wiped her eyes while she got control of herself.

"I'm sorry," Amy said. "We lost Paul and some of his troops early on. We don't know if they survived or not."

"I'm sorry," Ruth said. "I did not know."

"I hope we can go look for him now," Amy said.

Ruth looked at Amy. "I think we can help," she said. "Do you know where he might be?"

"Yes," Amy said. "He and his troops were surrounded in a farmhouse out toward Marion. One of the members of his platoon who got out can tell us where."

"We should go there tomorrow," Harold said. He didn't look happy about the idea, though. Amy saw the worry cross his features.

"There are other reasons to look back over the countryside on the way to Asheville," Amy said. "Something has been driving the zombies. I'm guessing there is a reason somewhere either along the way or in Asheville. We've come across the leftovers from Satan before, and I'm betting something is in Asheville." She looked at Harold and he now registered surprise and confusion. And he was looking behind Amy.

She spun around and coming across the parking lot were eight of the undead. No one had a blaster stick or other weapon, but Amy pulled up her bandana, slipped the sai out of her belt loops, and prepared to fight. She spun to her left and took two out right away. Then she kicked one out of her way, took another down striking up under the chin, then she finished off the one she kicked.

As she moved, the zombies turned her direction. *This just confirms that they are driven*, she thought. She drove a sai into the eye of number five. Number six, though, shifted as she tried to strike, and she missed. It reached for her, but Amy spun away. She ended number seven and eight quickly and turned back to six. It continued to shamble toward her, arms outstretched.

Amy brought the sai up and shoved the long tang into its head.

She looked around the parking lot while getting control of her breathing. There was no other movement. She guessed the group came out of the trees to the northwest, but nothing else seemed to be moving in that area. Zombie fluids dripped from the sai as she stood there. She pulled off her bandana and wiped off the sai, then threw the bandana into a trash bin near the truck.

"You are very ... surprising," Harold said as he and Ruth came up to Amy.

"I don't know what to say to that," Amy said. She smiled a small smile. "Thanks."

The zombies had normal clothing such as jeans, t-shirts, blouses, shorts, sneakers. It was almost like they were living their lives one moment, then turned into undead the next. Except for the aroma and rotting characteristics of their skin. Where there were wounds or injuries, the flesh was hanging in strips. There was no healing and no bleeding, just open festering wounds.

This was the closest Amy had been to the zombies long enough to see the details. She could see that one was once a boy of about fifteen. Number eight was a woman of maybe twenty-five. Whatever life they had before was over. Now their bodies could rest as well.

"Whatever did this to these people, we have to find it and end it," Amy said.

#

The fight against the zombie horde, Amy saw, was now reduced to perimeter patrols around the Raleigh area with help from the aliens. Every once in a while, patrols found a zombie wandering around, but even those incidents became rarer by the next day.

"But, we need to find Paul," she told Elder Franklin, Brad, and James as the troops stood down. "And we need to see if these zombies are still a problem in the Asheville area." She kept her suspicions of a driving force behind the horde to herself. "Harold offered a couple of saucers to scout through to where Paul was last seen and then on to Asheville."

Elder Franklin nodded as Amy spoke, then looked at Brad and James.

"We have a lot of work to do here," the elder said. "This fight against the zombies has taken a lot of people from the community during a time when we need people the most. Gardens need tending, buildings need maintenance and repair, and we need help getting our new friends settled in."

"We can send Amy, Sgt. Flynn, Lucy and a few of the mountain troops in two saucers with some of our new friends on this mission," James said. "The aliens'—we have to find a new word for them—communication is much better than our old radios. We can keep in touch with them. If something comes up, we can quickly mobilize to respond if they need help."

Brad nodded agreement. "They are still dismantling their starship. I understand they estimate this may take a couple of months. But there are a lot of very neat new tools and technologies they will share with us, so I'm hoping we can send some people up with them to learn and help."

"I want to get the people from the McGuire Nuclear Station that we brought back to connect with the aliens and learn about their power source," James said. "I suspect I know what it is, but I think experts should talk to them. Also, there are more folks at the New Hill facility, the Shearon Harris Nuclear Power Plant."

"One of the patrols can swing by and pick them up," Brad offered. "I'll talk to Ruth and see if our nuclear power folks can talk to their power system folks."

"When can we leave to find Paul?" Amy asked.

"It looks like as soon as Harold can gather you all together," Elder Franklin said. "I wish you Godspeed and hope you find Paul soon."

Amy stood to leave. "Thanks," she said. "We'll stay in touch."

She left the community hall and found Harold and Ruth sitting on a bench in the sun talking.

"We can go," she told Harold. "We need to gather Sgt. Flynn, Lucy, a few of the Asheville soldiers, and any of your people you want to bring."

"Very good," Harold said, standing. "I will have those of our people who will go meet us at the shuttles. I will see you there soon." He turned and left.

"Ruth," Amy said, "the elder and the others have some questions for you. I hope you don't mind me taking Harold away for a day or so."

"I don't mind," Ruth said. "I hope you find your Paul. I know he means a lot to you."

"Thank you, Ruth."

Amy headed to the west perimeter entrance and found Flynn and Lucy.

"So, we're good to go, Sgt. Flynn," Amy said. "Harold is getting the saucers ready. We need some troops from your outfit, and Harold is bringing some of his people."

"Amy, please call me Ron," Flynn said, grinning. "The captain just disbanded the unit, and we're all civilians now, working with the community. We're just dressed this way because it is all we have."

"Okay, Sgt. ... Ron," she said, dragging the name out. "It'll take some getting used to."

Lucy laughed. "Yeah, he does take a little getting used to." She poked Ron's side.

"So, do we have some of your former troops to help?"

"Yes," Ron said. "I have five tapped to come along. I'll go get them and meet you at the saucers."

Ron grabbed Lucy in a quick hug and kissed her, then left.

Lucy spun around smiling.

Amy laughed. "You like him a little bit?"

"Yeah," she said. "Just a little."

Amy led Lucy off to the saucers.

#

Amy studied the screen as Harold flew the saucer low and slow across the North Carolina countryside, not following any particular road, but heading toward Salisbury. From there, Amy thought they would follow US 70 through Statesville and Conover. Then they would cover the terrain straight to the farmhouse Paul was last seen.

"There's one," Amy said, pointing where the screen showed a zombie shambling along a side road.

Harold flicked his hands over the hemisphere and hit the firing button once and the zombie disappeared.

That was the third one they'd seen since leaving the Raleigh area. Amy suspected they would see more random solos and small clusters wandering around.

The other saucer was out to their left, according to Harold, flying low and slow just as they were. Amy watched as much for zombies as for humans. If Paul had managed to get his group free from the horde and was trying to get home, she didn't want to miss him. And she didn't want to blast him.

The saucer was traveling a little faster than a Humvee could go over the roads, but it was slower than Amy wanted to go. She originally wanted to go straight to the farmhouse, blast away at any zombies still there, and find Paul. Elder Franklin had convinced her that protecting the entire community was as important as finding Paul. The rescue mission could accomplish more by cleaning up the horde remnants as they went and maybe finding other survivors.

And she saw one. A survivor. Someone was moving along Alston Chapel Road west of Pittsboro. The person was carrying what looked like a shotgun. As they flew closer, the person stopped and looked up at the saucer, shading their eyes with a free hand.

"Let's drop a little closer," Amy said. Harold brought the saucer lower, closer to the tree tops. The person just watched and didn't raise the shotgun.

"Should we land and pick him up?" Lucy asked, coming up behind Amy.

"The person doesn't seem to be afraid of us," Amy said. "We probably should. Harold?"

Harold nodded and brought the saucer down next to the road. As soon as the gear was on the ground, he lowered the ramp.

"Lucy," Amy said, "let's go out and meet him or her."

The person turned out to be a young boy about fifteen years old.

"I saw you guys coming along and trying to fight the zombies," he said. "I tried to join up with y'all, but you moved too fast and blew some of the bridges."

"What's your name?" Lucy asked.

"Jeremy, ma'am," he said. "Can I join up with y'all now?"

The boy looked skinny and hungry to Amy, and she wasn't about to leave him alone out here.

"Still have ammo for that shotgun?" she asked.

"No, ma'am," Jeremy said. "I'm all out. I just keep this handy for a club." He showed her the butt of the gun, smeared with zombie fluids. "'Bout all it's good for now."

"Oh, well you can leave that here now," Amy said. "Come on up with us."

"Wow," Jeremy said, "I can't believe I'm gonna get to ride in a flying saucer!"

"I bet you're hungry, aren't you, Jeremy?" Lucy asked.

"Yes, ma'am," he agreed.

Lucy saw to it that Jeremy got a good MRE once inside the saucer. Harold drew up the ramp and they took off again.

Amy didn't see any more survivors, but they did spot a few more zombies and blasted them. Jeremy came over to the control console after eating his MRE. He was amazed at the saucer and Harold and watched every move Harold made. He even beat Amy at pointing out a zombie on the screen a few times. He asked a continual stream of questions, and Harold patiently answered them.

"I bet I could run this thing," Jeremy said. "It seems so easy!"

"That might be in your future," Amy said. "It really isn't hard. But it does belong to Harold and his people, so it will be up to them."

"Oh, cool," Jeremy said. "I'm kinda hungry again."

Amy looked at the skinny kid and smiled. "It must be about noon, isn't it?" she asked Lucy.

"Yeah," Lucy said.

Amy checked the screen. They were approaching Statesville.

"Harold, let's land in the open area by that interchange, there," she said. "We'll get some lunch and take a break before moving on."

SIXTEEN

Rescue

"Harold," Amy said as they ate sitting outside near the saucers. "What do you call yourselves?"

"Ourselves?"

"You know, like, we call ourselves humans, or people." She looked at Harold, then at the other aliens sitting around eating.

"Our word for ourselves," Harold said, "is much like yours. I think it translates much the same. We have a different genetic history on our home planet, so we aren't 'primates' as you are." He looked thoughtful for a moment. "Our word is," and he said the word in his native language.

Amy knew she would not be able to duplicate what he said. She wasn't even certain it was one word or more. But, part of it did sound a little like 'toast.' Well, she didn't think they could be called toast, that would be weird. The word host is close, but she didn't think that would fit, either. They came at first as enemies, but became friends. They helped and were helped. They shared and graciously accepted sharing.

The thing is, Amy thought, they will probably give more than we can ever repay.

"I think I have a name we can call you instead of alien," Amy finally concluded. "I don't like to call you 'alien' anymore because we've accepted you in our family, our community. You are not alien anymore. We'll call you 'patron' or 'patrons' as that seems to fit."

Harold thought about that for a moment, then nodded. "I like that. We have a word in our language for you, now. It is similar. It doesn't reference your biological category, just our relationship to you. It means friends."

"Good," Amy said. "Now we both have words to reference each other that mean basically the same thing."

He nodded and smiled, then spoke to the rest of the patrons in their native tongue to explain the dialogue. Soon, all were nodding and smiling.

Father, Amy prayed silently, *thank you for this great gift of the patrons. Thank you for helping turn my heart for them, and thank you for your blessings. Please, help me find Paul and his troops, and find them well and whole. I ask this in the name of your son, Jesus. Amen.*

After lunch, they loaded back into the saucers and floated west again.

Amy spotted, and Harold blasted the occasional zombie, but they found no other survivors wandering around. Jeremy, the only one they'd found, napped with some of the others on the floor of the saucer.

The terrain became hillier, and they had to increase their altitude a little to compensate for the rises and falls of the land. Interstate 40 tracked across the country to their north. Amy thought they were coming near the area where Paul and his people were last seen, so she brought up one of the troops who knew the location.

"How close are we?"

The troop looked at the screen. "We're still a ways out. See the power line right of way?" He pointed to the line of power transmission towers that marched across the country along a clear, treeless path just south of them. "That will cross the South Mountain Scenery Road, then the house will be right in front of you. When we had to leave, it was surrounded by zombies in the clearing around it."

Amy nodded. As she observed the terrain move below them on the screen, she saw the power line make a slight right just after it intersected with another going north and south.

"We're close," the troop said. "It'll cross the road in a minute."

A road just beneath them wound through small rural communities then ended at a junction.

"That's it," the troop said. "That's South Mountain Scenery." He watched the screen, then pointed. "There's the house."

"Okay," Amy said. "Get everyone geared up and ready."

She noted the house was surrounded by a lot of zombies still, but there were a lot of bodies scattered around the house as well.

"Let's swing around on the south side and blast away what we can without hitting the house," Amy said. Harold tapped his collar button and spoke a few words, then banked the saucer around to the south. Then he moved toward the house blasting zombies in the clearing.

As they blasted zombies, more flooded into the clearing from the surrounding woods. Harold banked the saucer around on the north side of the house and swept back across the clearing, blasting away. The other saucer was doing the same. More zombies flooded back in to the clearing. Smoke rose from the ground from the burned and blasted bodies and vegetation.

Two more passes, and the numbers of zombies flooding back into the clearing ebbed to a trickle. Another pass, and the zombies were almost gone. The house was still surrounded by a layer of zombies beating on the side of the building and the doors and boarded up windows. The layer was about three or four zombies deep.

"Okay," Amy said, "we'll have to get out and clear out that last bit."

Harold landed the saucer in an open field to the south of the house and lowered the ramp.

"Let's go," Amy said to the rest of the group as she ran down the ramp.

Tree stumps smoldered between the saucers and the house where the blasters had consumed trees and zombies during their passes.

She drew up her blaster stick and pointed toward the house.

"Shoot the zombies, not the house," she said to the group, as she waved them into a line to advance on the house. She noticed Ron was forming up the troops from the other saucer to her left. When she turned back from forming up her troops, the zombies were starting to break from the house and move in her direction.

She waited until her line had advanced almost to the smoldering stumps, then started firing on the zombies. The zombies were close, but the blasters hit them and not the house.

Ron moved his troops across the clearing to the left and thought to flank the zombies at the house. But as they started to fire on them, more zombies appeared out of the woods to the west.

"Behind you, Ron!" Amy shouted. Zombies started turning from the house and moving toward Ron's group. She immediately directed her group to fire on those zombies.

Ron's group turned and fired at the zombies coming out of the woods.

Amy managed to sweep her group up the west side of the house, clearing the zombies and keeping them from Ron's group. She directed fire against the zombies on the north and south side of the house, then she saw more coming out of the woods to the east.

Was this a trap? She looked around. A steady wave of zombies came out of the woods to the west, and a flood was cutting off escape to the north and east. They could try to run back south, but not everyone would make it.

Harold solved part of her problem. Both saucers were airborne again and sweeping across the woods on the west and east sides. The blasters took out trees and zombies indiscriminately. On the north side, they converged fire to sweep the incoming driveway and woods.

Amy and Ron kept the troops firing at any zombies entering the clearing. The saucers swept back across the burned out woods. Then they turned and made another sweep further out on each side. Soon, Amy and Ron stood with their troops watching the saucers pass. There were no more zombies to blast.

#

Amy slowly walked up to the door on the north side of the house. She hadn't seen any movement in the open second floor windows. She suspected Paul and his troops used those as firing positions for as long as they had ammo. She stepped across a smoldering zombie body.

The door, like the first floor windows, was boarded up. Zombie fluids covered it where they had pushed up and pounded on it for days. There were fluids smeared all across the lower part of the siding, as well.

"Blast the door," Amy said. "Don't touch it. Let's just burn it away."

One of the troops fired and a huge smoking hole replaced the door.

Tools, lumber and furniture were scattered around the main room. A staircase led up on the right. On the left the room opened into the kitchen and dining area. It was dark, since all the windows were boarded up. Amy waved a couple of troops toward the kitchen.

"Make sure we're clear down here."

She then led the others slowly up the stairs. At the top, she directed two to go right and she went left. She passed a bathroom and then entered a large bedroom. Two people were on the bed, and another was propped against the wall under the window. They all had their weapons close, but none moved.

Amy crept close. They smelled, but it was just body odor. The young man under the window seemed to be sleeping. She looked at the two men on the bed. The first one was Paul!

She immediately moved next to him and put her hand on his chest.

"Paul," she said quietly, "Paul. Wake up."

Paul's eyes slowly opened. His eyes were clear, but she could tell he was weak. He tried to speak, but she put her finger on his lips. She looked around the room. There were no trash piles from MREs, just empty ammo magazines and spent cartridges littering the floor.

"Oh, my," she said. "They are starving and probably haven't had any water in days!"

She called out her find.

"We have three more in the other room," a troop said coming to the door. "Alive, but barely."

"Gather the blankets and let's make some litters," Amy said. "Get these people into the saucers."

Ron's group had stayed outside as security, and it was a good thing. More zombies showed up, but they were random solos or small groups. Amy directed the activities getting Paul and his people out of the house and into the saucers.

"Let's get back to the community," Amy told Harold when everyone was loaded and being cared for in the saucers. "As fast as we can safely go."

Harold tapped his collar button and said a few words, then fired up the saucer, raised the ramp and they were on their way.

All of Paul's people were awake now and getting sips of water.

"You found us," Paul croaked when Amy got near. A patron helping Paul gave him another sip of water from a canteen. "We didn't give up. I prayed for you to come."

Amy bent over and kissed him lightly.

"There was no doubt I would come back for you."

Paul smiled weakly. Amy looked him over. His hollow cheeks and sunken eyes from lack of food and water made him look near dead.

"Let's see if we can get them some protein and carbs," Amy suggested to the patron. Just then another patron came by with some hot meatloaf and crackers. "You guys read my mind."

They helped Paul get a few bites of each. He chewed slowly and swallowed. The patron took the food to another troop. Then Paul took another sip of water.

"I feel like I just had a huge meal," he said.

"Rest, now," Amy said.

Paul smiled and closed his eyes. He fell asleep, breathing easily.

Thank you, Father, she prayed. *Thank you for helping me find Paul.*

When she looked up, the patron helping Paul smiled at her. He reached out and put a hand on her shoulder and gave a gentle squeeze.

"Thank you," she said.

When she stood, she could feel Harold was bringing the saucer down to land. Were they back at the community already? She went to the control console and looked at the screen. They were back at the landing fields next to the west perimeter of the community.

Harold had called ahead, and people were waiting to help get Paul and his troops into the health clinic.

#

Paul still looked a little haggard, Amy thought, but he was mobile and talking. That was good. It took a couple of days to rehydrate and feed the men they brought back.

"How did you guys survive?" Amy asked when they had some alone time.

"The house had a lot of lumber stacked in the garage," he explained. "We used what tools we could find to board the windows and doors on the first floor. Then we stayed on the second floor. We shot them until we ran out of ammo. Otherwise, we tried to keep calm, conserve our energy, and not get too hot. Thank God the zombies couldn't climb."

"It looked like they tried," Amy said, thinking about the way the house was smeared all along the outside walls.

"Yeah," he nodded. "We got to where we just ignored them. They couldn't get to us, so why worry? Food and water became a problem after a day or so. What little we had with us was gone in hours. There was nothing in the house. You showed up at the last possible minute. If you'd come the next day, I think you would have just found our bodies."

Amy described what they found when they arrived, then what happened after several sweeps.

"It was like they set a trap for us," Amy said. "I know that sounds paranoid, but that's what it looked like. If it wasn't for Harold, we might have been caught in it."

"Yeah, about those aliens," Paul said, his face reflecting his anger and concern. "When did they show up?"

Amy brushed her hands through her hair and pulled it back over her shoulders.

"Well, we call then patrons now. Alien just didn't seem right," she said. "We'd been pushed back and would have been wiped out at Raleigh if they hadn't shown up. At first, I thought we had another enemy."

She explained the meeting of the patrons, the change in their leadership since she and Paul fought them in Montana and Wyoming, and that they were desperate to get off their failing starship.

"They joined our fight. Harold said if they didn't, they would die too. But, Paul," Amy touched his arm, "they are wonderful and have done so much to help. Please have an open mind."

Paul looked at Amy for a moment. Doubt clouded his face. She could see the pain reflected in his eyes, and she knew he was remembering Joe.

"A lot has happened since Joe, Paul," Amy said. "A lot to us and a lot to them. Give them a chance to share their story. Harold's wife, Ruth, is the leader."

Paul finally nodded and took her hand. "I will," he said. "There's been too much loss, pain, and suffering. It needs to end."

"Good," she said. "I'm going to work out. I'll be back to take you to a meeting with the leaders in a couple of hours."

"Okay."

"Get some more food and rest." She kissed him. "I love you."

SEVENTEEN

Source

Amy and Paul entered the community hall and found a place to sit among the people and patrons gathered. Elder Franklin and James Carson sat at a table on the stage with Harold and Ruth. The elder checked the time, then stood.

"I'll bring this to order now," he said. "We have some information to share and decisions to make. James."

The room quieted, and James stood. A map of North Carolina was hung behind him and James pointed to the area of Asheville.

"Ron Flynn and John Wilkerson gave me as much information as they knew about the zombies and Asheville," he began. "From their reports, Harold and the patrons working on the starship ran a scan across Asheville and the surrounding area. They'd been able to see the huge mass of zombies moving across the state before they landed. So, before they completely dismantled that part of the ship, we had them run this task."

He tried to point with his right hand, but something was jammed on his prosthetic and he couldn't. He slipped his left hand into his shirt and fiddled with something, then took it out and pulled the prosthetic off and laid it on the table.

"Sorry, it's been giving me a little trouble," he said, then smiled. "I'm glad we have Paul back. He can help me fix it."

There was some light laughter in the room. Amy noticed Harold and Ruth staring at the prosthetic arm. They had a brief conversation then paid attention to what James said.

"What we have," James continued, "is an area still infested with zombies. There is something just east of downtown Asheville, and the zombies seem to center on that. Best we can tell, it is in a cemetery out on New Leicester Highway.

"Now, thanks to the patrons, we managed to give mercy to thousands, probably tens of thousands, of zombies. But, we still have some in Asheville. If this thing in the cemetery is the source of them, we need to take it out and clean up the last of the zombies."

"Naelchel said there were more," Amy whispered to Paul as James sat. They'd confronted the demon Naelchel in Washington, D.C. "Do you suppose this is another demon?"

"I don't know," he said. "If it is, we are very poorly equipped to deal with it. But I would guess it is something else. Remember, God doesn't give us a challenge we can't meet. That doesn't mean it will be easy."

Harold stood and looked at the people in the room.

"We have completed dismantling all the system on our big ship," he said. "Only the shell remains. It will stay in orbit for some time, and we can cut it up as we need materials. So, we have our immediate critical needs met and can dedicate all our shuttles to finishing this. There are enough we may be able to surround the infestation and burn it out."

Heads nodded across the room.

"But," Harold continued, "people and patrons should be on the ground to insure it is complete. We do not know what is at the center of this. That may be a big fight."

Harold returned to his seat and talk scattered across the room.

James stood again. "The plan is to leave early in the morning tomorrow and fly as quickly as we can to Asheville in the saucers. Each saucer will have a full complement of troops. They will drop the troops at key locations and begin to sweep across the area. The troops will move through and mop up random solo or small groups, or direct saucer firepower if they discover larger groups."

James looked around the room.

"We must be cautious," he said. "Whatever is directing the zombies isn't stupid. Our rescue of Paul and his people, we think, was a trap—of sorts. Our people managed to beat it, but still, it was a trap. Be wary, be prepared, and be careful."

James covered a few more details of the operation, and the meeting broke up.

"Get a good sleep tonight," Elder Franklin said as people started to leave.

Amy walked out of the hall on Paul's arm. Harold and Ruth followed.

"The patrons aren't going to stay in the dorms forever, are they?" Amy asked. "There are still a lot of houses around here that aren't being used."

"No, not forever," Ruth said. "Elder Franklin and I have talked about it. After we remove this evil thing in Asheville, we will start working on the houses and moving our people into them as they get finished."

"Well, the dorms were just a temporary, emergency setup," Amy said. "Getting you into houses will really help get things normal."

"Oh, normal will take some time," Ruth said. "That is expected. We have a lot of work to do and things to build. We have a lot of things to teach, too."

Paul looked at Ruth and Harold. "Oh?"

"We'll go over that when we have time," Harold said. "We all have our priorities."

"Yeah, I guess we do," Paul said.

Amy hugged his arm a little tighter. "I got my Paul back, so that was my first priority," she said.

#

Amy moved in the dark with Paul, heading for the assembly area. The sun hadn't come up yet.

"Are you sure you should be going?" Amy said. "You're still a little weak."

"I'm fine. I wouldn't miss this. And I don't want to be away from you." He looked at his gear. "Besides, we have water, food, and these blaster sticks don't weigh anything. No problem."

"It better be no problem," she said and punched his shoulder.

"Ouch!"

James and Brad were sorting people into the six saucers and directing the loading of supplies. Each team had one person with an M-4 carbine with the sniper scope. Lucy had her bow slung on her back. Amy had her sai. Everyone else, except the saucer drivers, had blaster sticks.

"We're loaded up, everyone into your saucer," James said. He patted Brad on the back with his left hand and watched as everyone else went into a saucer.

Amy saw James' face. She felt he really wanted to go. As good as his prosthetics were, he couldn't keep up with the others, and his phantom pain convulsions weren't under control. He'd long ago run out of pain medicine, and the TENS machine wasn't enough. He struggled through it, and she knew how hard he worked to keep a stoic face in front of everyone.

Ruth walked up to James just as Amy got up the ramp and lost sight of him.

"James is hurting," Amy told Paul.

"Yeah, I know," he said. "I helped him for a while last night on the arm. The elbow and hand joints are wearing out and jamming. The leg isn't going to last much longer, either. I had to solder one of the knee joints brackets back in place. And he had two episodes while I was there."

"I wish there was something we could do for him," she said.

Paul nodded.

Amy walked over to the console and watched the screen as Harold piloted the saucer in formation with the other five. The terrain sped by under them.

"How soon should we be there?" she asked.

"Soon," Harold responded. "Before morning. We will move around the city and position ourselves so we can attack the zombies before the daylight comes."

She realized Harold had trouble expressing time in human terms. *It's probably a language thing,* she thought.

The terrain speeding by under them changed, and a few minutes later, Harold banked the saucer into a sweeping turn to the north. He tapped the screen a couple of times, and it changed to the night vision style she'd seen before.

Harold oriented the saucer to its place in the formation that surrounded Asheville and slowed to a seeming walking pace. The screen displayed the terrain, with woods, gardens, fields, buildings, and roads in a glowing negative style. No zombies appeared yet.

Amy looked back at Paul and smiled. She hoped this operation would go well and quickly and they could go home and just *be home*. Paul smiled back at her. A warmth welled up in her. Maybe she would not make him wait to get married. At this point, she wondered what purpose waiting served.

Harold stopped the saucer and lowered the ramp. "Zombies ahead," he said, then tapped his collar and spoke in his language.

Paul paused at the top of the ramp and looked at Harold.

"We will cover your movement for now," Harold said. "The zombies are ahead about 100 of your meters. They just shift around. No directed movement. I don't think they realize we are here."

"Thanks, Harold." Paul said. He pulled out his map and moved quickly down the ramp.

The ramp rose and closed on the saucer, then it quickly lifted off and moved toward the zombies.

Paul waved their team into a line and led them in the same direction. Amy kept close to Paul.

Amy saw the saucer slow ahead, and then the blaster swept across an area to its front. The bright glow from the blaster briefly lit the area, and they saw forms shambling around in a large group until they were blasted to ashes.

"We should watch our flanks," Amy told Paul. "They may be just stumbling around in the dark right now, but a solo may come out from the woods or behind a building." He nodded and passed the word through the team.

Of course, Amy thought, as a solo came stumbling out from behind a building on their left, *I would have to jinx it.*

The patron on the left end of the line spun, fired, and dropped the zombie.

Paul kept the line moving as the saucer swept zombies away in front of them.

Day dawned as they continued to slowly move against the zombies. When the light was good, Paul looked at his map and got oriented.

"We're moving directly against that ... well ... whatever it is in that cemetery," he said.

Amy looked ahead where the saucer continued to blast at zombies.

"They are getting thicker," she said.

Just then, one of their team on the right blasted a solo that appeared out of some trees. Then the patron on the left fired again, dropping another zombie.

Paul tapped a nearby patron on the shoulder. "Call Harold, see if he can sweep our flanks," he said.

The patron tapped his collar and spoke.

"He will do that," the patron said.

"Hold here, then," Paul said.

The saucer came around to their left, sweeping the blaster across houses and yards, then it swung around behind them and swept up the right and blasted away at the open woods.

"We should be clear now," the patron told Paul.

"Tell Harold, thanks," Paul said. The patron nodded, and Paul waved the team forward.

"We have a long way to go," Paul said to Amy. "It's a little over three kilometers to the cemetery from here. At this rate, it will be after noon before we get there."

#

Amy blasted several zombies that moved their direction. The team on the left and right were fully engaged. She and Paul, with the rest of the team in the center, were firing almost constantly. The sniper, Joshua, just to Amy's right, had given up on using the carbine since there were so many coming at them, and the range was too close. He'd slung the carbine and pulled out the blaster stick.

Harold was up there firing away with the saucer's blaster, and it wasn't slowing down the horde at all.

Paul tapped the patron next to him.

"Can we get more help here?" he asked. "See if everyone is getting this much pressure."

The patron tapped his collar button and talked. A few seconds later he got back to Paul, between firing at zombies. "The other teams are seeing very few zombies. They continue to advance. Three are clearing out the main part of the city, and those saucers are needed. Two saucers are sent to us to help. They should be here soon."

"Relay my thanks," Paul said and resumed firing.

Amy didn't notice if the patron relayed the message, she was busy blasting away. The blaster stick was getting warm.

"We're still more than two klicks from the cemetery," Paul said. "And man, this stick is getting hot."

Amy saw Harold burn down a large group of zombies coming through a bunch of mobile homes. Then the saucer swung to the right and blasted across the large body of zombies moving down the road among the trees and homes to their south.

Then the two other saucers joined the fight. One was out on the highway, blasting away at enemies Amy couldn't see. The other pulled up next to Harold, and the two combined their fire on the horde to the south.

That took the pressure off the team, so Paul waved them forward again. Amy fired at anything the saucers left for them.

As they moved down the road, Amy could see more out to the highway after the saucers burned away the trees and buildings. New Leicester Highway was packed with zombies coming their way. *At least we have three saucers helping with this mess,* she thought. But, they were making progress. The team was able to clean up after the saucers sweeps, and the main horde was getting thinned down.

I'm not shooting as often, and the stick isn't as hot, she thought.

She pushed alongside Paul, and the team moved out onto the highway. The horde was thinning, and the saucers were keeping up a voracious fire that took the pressure off the team. They were able to move along a little faster, past the burnt trees and homes along the highway. Fewer and fewer zombies came at them from the flanks, so they were able to concentrate their fire on what was ahead.

Progress swung the team down the highway and around a bend. Amy could see radio towers poking out above the trees on her left. What was left of a neighborhood thick with trees was on her right. Now it was a smoldering landscape, dotted with piles of ash.

The saucers were spread out more now as the horde thinned, and they were able to apply their fire across a larger area. The team almost trotted down the road, firing on the move.

Amy saw a pawn shop sign on the right next to the smoldering remains of a building. More structures ahead and to the left were burnt to the ground, or falling to ruin after getting partially blasted.

Paul checked the map. "We're less than a kilometer out," he announced. "We don't know what we're running into, so let's slow it down a little."

The team obliged and slowed to a walk. Paul tapped the patron next to him.

"Ask Harold what we have up ahead," he said.

The patron tapped his collar button and spoke. He listened, then spoke again.

"Harold said it is evil up there. Big evil."

"What's the status of the rest of the teams?"

"They are all approaching this location." The patron waved in the general direction of the cemetery. "Carefully."

"So, all six saucers will be here?"

The patron nodded.

"Ask Harold to hold until we catch up," Paul said, then turned to the team. "Let's catch up to the saucers."

Amy ran alongside Paul, shooting the occasional zombie, until they caught up with the saucers at the edge of the cemetery. The saucers had already burned away most of the trees near the road, so their view into the cemetery was unobstructed.

The grounds of the cemetery rose in gentle slopes to a hilltop. A small pond was tucked into the slope near the front. But at the top of the hill something pulsed and glowed. There were many colors scrambled into the bulging dome-like thing. It resembled an infection. A puss-filled blister on the earth.

As she watched, Amy saw a zombie eject from the body of the blister and stumble around. Someone immediately fired and blasted it to ash.

"Well," Amy said, "at least it isn't a demon."

"But, it is evil," the patron said. "Very big evil. I can feel it."

"What happens if we fire on it?" Paul asked.

The patron spoke into the collar radio. There followed a short pause, then all six saucers fired on the blister. They stopped, and wounds appeared in the blister, but they healed right away. Two more zombies ejected from the side of the blister.

"Try again," Paul said. "Sweep across it."

The patron spoke and a moment later the saucers fired. This time, they swept the beams across the blister.

Wounds appeared again, but healed. Amy thought the blister looked smaller, and four more zombies ejected from it.

"They should keep firing," Amy said. "And we should move up on it and fire."

Paul nodded.

"Tell them to keep firing," Paul said. "Let's move up."

The saucers poured blaster fire into the blister. It took longer to heal, but zombies ejected from its sides. The teams burnt them away as they approached. Then, they were close enough, and everyone in the teams opened fire.

Between the saucer fire and the teams, the blister began to break up and collapse. Zombies ceased to emerge from it. Amy moved closer as it shrank and kept firing.

EIGHTEEN

Asheville

At the bottom of the crater left behind by the blister Amy saw a round, black sphere of what looked like glass. The saucer blasters deflected from it and hit the dirt and rocks surrounding it.

"Stop firing," Paul told the team.

The crater, Amy guessed, was about fifty meters across and twenty deep. The sphere in the bottom was about the size of a large car. The blasters were ineffective. She picked up a rock about the size of her fist and threw it. It bounced off, but she thought she heard a crack when it hit.

"Throw rocks at it," Amy said. She picked up another rock and threw it. She heard another crack.

Others threw rocks and the cracks heard were louder and louder. Soon, the cracks were like shrieks and the glass-like sphere split apart and exploded into thousands of pieces. The shards scattered across the filthy floor of the crater, and swirling colors reflected off the shards' cracked surfaces.

Amy started to move closer to some of the shards to get a better look.

"Amy, stop," a nearby patron shouted. "Please. Don't touch. Don't go near. Evil still."

She stopped and looked around. The patrons were trying to get everyone back out of the crater. Harold came up.

"Please, Amy," he said. "Come back up. Away from those."

He gently pulled on her arm, and she reluctantly followed.

"I just wanted to get a closer look at them," she said.

"Yes," he said. "But you must not. It is still evil."

Harold tapped the button on his collar and spoke. After a moment he nodded, then spoke again. Then he looked at Amy and Paul.

"We have our transports bringing some equipment," Harold said. "This is the evil that caused the enemy here. It is broken, but still evil. We cannot touch it. But, we can make it so it cannot do more harm."

"How will you do that?" Paul asked.

"We will bury it." Harold looked around the rim of the crater. "For now, we should watch and wait. Maybe have lunch. The transports are not as fast as the shuttles."

Amy and Paul laughed at that, knowing how quickly the saucers got to Asheville that morning. Paul went to find Brad to relay what Harold said. Amy sat on a large, rectangular grave marker.

"How do you know it is evil," Amy asked Harold. He sat next to her on the marker.

"We can ... feel it," he said. "It is not from here. Not from our reality."

"I think Satan put it here during The Troubles," Amy said. "We saw zombies here in Asheville when we came through . We managed to escape then."

"This Satan, he has some other names," Harold said.

"Yes. The Adversary—when we don't want to name him directly. Lucifer was his name when he was one of God's favorite angels. Sometimes, he's called Beelzebub or Ba'al. The Devil."

"I know some of the story," he said. "We read your Holy Bible. We have much to discuss and much to understand. Some of us have found names we like there."

"That's what we thought," Amy said smiling at the patron. "We think that is very special. But, where did you find 'Harold' for a name?"

"I read some old histories we found," he said. "They were about Danes, Vikings, and Norsemen. Harold, in different forms, was the name of many leaders in those histories. I liked it."

"It's a good name," she nodded. *Odd*, she thought, *how someone coming here from the outside just gets bits and pieces.* "What else did you read?"

"Not very much. The Holy Bible, those histories, some magazines and newspapers. Not as much as I would have liked. After what you call The Troubles, we were busy trying to get home, then trying to get rid of the bad leader, then keeping our big ship working."

Amy hadn't thought much about how hard life was for the patrons aboard a dying starship after a revolt, knowing you couldn't go home—and knowing that if you didn't do something, you would die in space. Now, as she looked at Harold, she saw the pain and loss in his eyes.

"You would rather have gone home," Amy said.

"Yes," he nodded. "Yes, it was the best choice, but we could not."

"What broke?"

"The ... navigation computer," Harold struggled with the right words. "The bad boss broke it when we would not do what he said. He thought we would ... agree with him if we could not go home."

"Oh."

"But, I think we were lost anyway," Harold said. "Reality was twisted, and we came here. We do not know how. So, it didn't really matter that bad boss broke the navigation."

"Well, I think you found a home here," Amy said. "We've lost so much. Without your help, the horde would have taken all of us. We'll need your help now to keep going."

"We need your help," Harold said. "We don't know how to make food here. None of us are ... farmers. Your weather is hard for us to understand. We saw big storms from up there. They scare us."

"It's part of our planet. We live with it. Sometimes it's hard, but we do okay."

Harold looked up, listening, then looked back at Amy.

"The transports are almost here," he said getting up. "I will get them landed. We can go home soon."

Harold paused and looked out past the destruction of Asheville and to the mountains. He made a small smile. "Yes. Home. I like that." Then he moved off.

#

Amy watched from the edge of the crater as Harold directed the transports to a landing area. Once on the ground, the large box-like flyers opened large bay doors, and two odd pieces of equipment moved out.

They moved on two wide, triangular shaped track belts. The main body was a square-shaped box with a large tube sticking out of one side. Amy thought it looked like a child's crayon drawing of a tank.

The two units moved slowly up the gentle slope, avoiding the grave markers until they stopped at the edge of the crater. Harold and the other patrons moved everyone back from the edge as a precaution.

A moment later, a whine rose from the machines, and then a white fluid began pouring from the tubes. It came slowly at first, but the whine deepened, and the flow came faster. Soon, the flow was shooting out of the tubes, and the fluid was cascading into the center of the crater.

Amy thought the fluid looked like thick cream, only whiter. It smashed into the center of the crater and began to cover the shards scattered across the bottom. She heard hissing and popping everywhere the fluid touched the shards. Then it began to fill the bottom of the crater.

"How much will you cover?" Amy asked Harold.

"We will bury this deep. When it is hard, no one will be able to get through it," he said. "It will keep the evil there." He pointed to the center of the crater. "It will not leave."

The machines continued to pour the white fluid into the crater, and it slowly rose. Soon, the crater was half full.

Paul and Brad came around the crater to where Amy stood with Harold.

"What is that stuff?" Paul asked.

"I don't know your word for it," Harold said. "But when we fill this, it will harden, and it will not break. That evil will stay there."

Amy noticed the fluid was beginning to curdle, like sour milk. What was in the crater was getting thicker, and it was almost to the edge. The whining from the machines started to lessen, and the flow from the tubes decreased and stopped.

As she watched, the white material got thicker and thicker, bulging in the center to make a slight dome over the crater. Then it was hard with a bright, white, smooth, gleaming finish.

She moved close to the edge and looked at the material. She could see her face in the mirror-like surface. She reached out and tapped it with her hand. It was hard as a rock and made no sound when she tapped on it.

Whatever those shards were, I think we stopped the evil, she thought.

Paul came up and banged on the surface with the butt of a combat knife. No sound, no vibration that Amy could tell. And the knife butt left no mark. Not a scratch.

"It is very hard," Harold said. "So, it is a good solution."

"Yes," Brad agreed. "I hope it holds."

"It will," Harold assured him.

Amy looked at Harold. "But, you can still feel the evil there, right?"

"Yes."

"Okay, let's pack this up and go home," Brad said.

#

The trip back to Raleigh was slower since they moved at the speed of the transports. It gave Amy some time to think, and then time to grill Harold. He seemed a little put off by her questions, but he answered.

"Those two machines," Amy queried, "where did all that stuff come from?"

"The machines made it."

"How did they make it?"

"They make it from," Harold waved his hand around in the air, "everything."

This still didn't connect for Amy. She thought some more.

"So, what is that material? How did you decide what to have the machines make?"

"We made settings to produce the correct material to contain the evil," Harold said. "This is not my skill."

"Oh, so you didn't program the machines?"

"No, I told our people what we needed. They sent the machines."

"So, do they know what that stuff is?"

"I don't think so. It is what came because of what we asked for."

"So, if I needed to reinforce a dam for example," Amy said, "I'd tell your people what I wanted, and they would send the machines ready to provide the material I needed?"

"Yes."

"How do they know what material to provide?"

"They don't. They tell the machine what is wanted. The machine provides the material."

Amy started getting the point. The patrons used the machines but had little direct understanding of how they worked. And they must have some kind of artificial intelligence.

"So, how does this saucer fly?"

Harold gave Amy a look like he might give an inquisitive three-year-old who asked too many questions.

"I push this button, and move this lever, and it flies."

"Do you know what makes it fly?"

Harold shook his head slowly. Amy thought he looked resigned to his fate.

"I do not know what makes it fly, no," he said quietly. "I know it has a ... motor, an engine. But, I know nothing about that or the systems. If we have damage or need repair, we bring in a machine and it does the repairs."

Amy sat quietly for a few moments. *This is interesting,* she thought. Harold could pilot the saucer, but knew nothing about the systems that made it work, made it fly. So, why were they not able to repair the navigation system on the starship? Or, fix the other systems that provided food and life support?

"So," she started, and Harold interrupted her.

"When we revolted against the bad boss, he destroyed our navigation computer," he said, and Amy heard some irritation in his voice. "It is ... complicated. He also broke some of the machines we used. We did not know how to ask our machines to make a new navigation computer. Or fix our life support."

"You are dependent on these machines to do most of the technical work for you," Amy said. "But you need to know how to make the request."

Harold nodded. "Yes, I think that is how you would say it."

"So, if you knew how to ask one of your machines how to make another saucer," she said, "you could make another saucer. Or, a transport."

He nodded again. "Yes, and many other things. Even engines."

"Harold, I don't mean to upset you," Amy said. "I'm just trying to understand. From our perspective, you have rather miraculous machines. We had a lot of things before The Troubles, but not anymore. We don't have the people or the infrastructure to build and maintain them." She held out her hands. "We have to build and fix the things we use. Ourselves. We don't have machines to do it for us."

A light seemed to come on in Harold's eyes, and he looked at Amy.

"I think I see," he said. "Without our machines, we don't know how to build, make, or fix things. We know how to use the machines, the saucers, the equipment. But that is it."

Amy smiled. "I think I have a better understanding, now."

The patrons came to the right place, Amy thought. *We can help them, they can help us.*

NINETEEN

Worship

When they landed near Raleigh, Amy came down the ramp with Paul. Brad was already talking with Elder Franklin and James, giving them a debrief on the operation. A man she thought she recognized as a member of the group from one of the nuclear power plants stood nearby, fidgeting. He seemed excited and about to burst out.

Elder Franklin introduced the man as George Larimore.

"This is one of the engineers from McGuire Nuclear Station," the elder said. "He has some interesting news."

George smiled and cleared his throat.

"We've been working with the patrons. They have some incredible technology. The most fascinating is their energy units. These are small, self-contained, completely shielded fusion reactors. They can run indefinitely and can be used to produce whatever material is needed from whatever they can feed into it."

He bounced on his feet a little in his excitement.

"These are the core units that power the saucers, the machines, the weapons, and they broadcast power to devices like the blaster sticks remotely. This was the dream of Nikola Tesla, if he had access to this kind of fusion reactor. The reactor is completely safe, no emissions."

"And their little machines can make more of them," Amy added.

George looked at her agape.

"I grilled Harold on the way home," she said grinning.

"I'm trying to pick their brains on the technology," George said. "It is fascinating."

"I'm afraid that won't do a lot of good," Amy said. "They know how to operate their machines and equipment, but they don't know the technology. They've had it so long, and it works so well, they don't need to know the nitty-gritty details."

George frowned. "So," he started, then stopped.

"That's where we come in," Amy said, Paul wrapped an arm around her. She looked up at him and saw the pride in his face. "We know how to take things apart and figure them out. We're good at that. The patrons can help us, but that part will be mostly up to us."

James stepped forward then. "So, you're saying we learn how the patron technology works and we in turn teach them?"

Amy nodded.

"This will change everything," Elder Franklin said. "A reliable source of power and transportation, machines to help make and maintain what we need." The elder shook his gray head and raised his hands to heaven. "Praise the Lord."

Nuclear power was not Amy's area, of course, but she saw the value of the fusion reactors that powered everything the patrons had and used. She also saw the bargain being struck to help the patrons. They arrived when the community was in a desperate state and willingly joined in to help bring an end to the horde and the evil behind it.

Without the patrons, Amy, Paul, and the entire community would be lost. Washington, D.C. would eventually be lost, as well. Maybe even the scattered survivors around the world. Now, with the help of the patrons, Amy felt they had a far better opportunity for survival.

#

"So," Amy asked Ruth as they walked toward the community market, "how long have you and Harold been married?"

"We were joined when we were very young. It is the practice of our people. Harold is a good person, and I love him very much."

"Did your parents arrange it, then?"

"No, it was, uh," Ruth paused and thought. "We were joined through a selection."

"Oh."

"You and Paul, you plan to become married?"

"Yes. I think it might be sooner than later," Amy said. She felt the color rise in her cheeks at the thought. "I'm looking forward to it."

"So, how were you selected?"

"Paul chose me. I chose him."

"Oh, you chose each other?"

"Yes."

"Hmmm ... " Ruth pondered that a moment. "Today, if I were to choose, I would choose Harold. But, I was very young when we were selected."

"Paul and I have been friends since we were very young," Amy said. "We've been best friends. I think that helped us make the right choice."

"How do you marry?"

"We have a ceremony. It's very beautiful, and God joins us together as one. We say vows to each other."

"God joins you?" Ruth looked surprised. "I read something about that in your Holy Bible. How is that? Does he attend the ceremony?"

"No," Amy smiled. "God joins us in our hearts, spiritually. Marriage for us is a holy ordinance."

Amy started picking out fresh produce at one of the stalls. She sniffed at a tomato, smiled and put it and several others like it in her basket. Then she saw some string beans.

"Do you have a ceremony for marriage?" Amy asked.

"No," Ruth said. "When we are selected, we are told we are joined and we touch hands. From then on, we are together."

"What if you don't like the person you are joined to?"

Ruth looked at Amy, her large eyes glistening in the sunshine. Amy could see her reflection in them. "I don't know. Some I know are not happy with their selection. But, they continue to live and work. So, I don't know that there is anything to do."

That seemed sad to Amy. "What about children?"

Ruth examined a bunch of asparagus then put it in her basket. "Some of us have children. On the big ship, we try to limit that because there is no space. Now, though, that might change."

"I want to have children," Amy said. "Not many, just a few."

Ruth smiled. "I have been thinking I might want to have a child. Harold would be a good father."

Amy and Ruth worked with the booth vendor to complete the trade. Amy still had gourds from last summer and winter carrots. Ruth offered a blanket she made with one of her machines. When the exchange was done, they moved on.

"I think it would be wonderful to see Harold as a father," Amy said. "He seems to be pretty good with some of the kids around here."

"Yes, he finds them fascinating."

Amy took a deep breath, smelling the summer scents of flowers and growing things. The pressure was off. The horde was gone. Life was almost back to normal. Tomorrow was Sunday. Worship.

"Ruth, would you and Harold come with Paul and I to worship service tomorrow?"

"Worship? What is that?"

"You read about Sabbath in The Bible," Amy said. "We observe Sabbath on Sunday. We join together as a community, sing, pray, and worship together. I would love it if you and Harold could join us."

"We will do that."

#

Amy heard the piano and singing starting as she and Paul approached the hall for worship. Ruth and Harold waited near the door for them and accompanied them into the hall.

They found seats and then sang along with the first two songs. Amy saw Harold and Ruth trying to sing along. They did seem to enjoy the music and the voices in unison.

The routine of the service was automatic for Amy and Paul. Harold and Ruth followed along.

After the singing and prayers, Pastor Andrew Smith got up to the podium and started teaching from the Beatitudes, Matthew chapter five, verses one through twelve.

"These verses, this teaching from Jesus, seems so appropriate at this point," Smith said after he read the verses and looked around the room. Both human and patron filled the hall. "We are welcoming friends whose help we needed, and who need our help. Jesus gave us these teachings to help us understand that what we give, we will receive. If we give love, we will receive love. If we comfort, we will be comforted.

"We do not do these things to enrich ourselves here on earth, in this world, but we do these things so that we find our rewards in heaven. This world is temporary. We find no lasting peace, no lasting reward here. We live our best life, we hope for the best, we make the best of what we have. Our best, brightest, most glorious reward, though, is when we get to rejoin Jesus."

Amy held Paul's hand while the pastor continued. Then she reached out and held Ruth's hand. *This is how it should be,* she thought as the pastor's voice rumbled in the background. *We do our best and make this the best we can make it.*

She glanced at Ruth, who smiled back.

"An interesting take on verse nine," Pastor Smith continued, "is that the Hebrew word for peace is 'Shalom.' This word means a number of things, like harmony, wholeness, prosperity. It can be used, like the Hawaiian 'Aloha', for hello and goodbye. But looking at this verse from this perspective: blessed are the peacemakers, blessed are the harmony makers, blessed are the prosperity makers, blessed are the wholeness makers.

"Look at each other and say, Shalom."

The congregation did, and the word Shalom flowed around the room.

"You are saying hello, goodbye, well met, be at peace, be in harmony, be whole, be prosperous. So, blessed are you who say Shalom, because you will be called children of God."

Smith turned to a small table near him and picked up a covered loaf of bread.

"So, this brings us to the table. The table that holds the gifts of God for the children of God." He uncovered the loaf and held it up. "On the night he was betrayed, he took up the loaf of hidden presence, broke it, and gave it to them. He said, 'Take it: this is my body.'"

He set the broken loaf back on the tray and picked up a small pitcher and a cup and held them up. "Then he took the cup of the fruit of the vine and said, 'This is my blood of the new covenant, which is poured out for many.'"

He poured the juice into the cup and set them down on the tray.

"For when you take this bread and drink this cup, you proclaim the Lord's death and the forgiveness of sin until the day he returns."

As the elders approached to serve communion, Amy and Paul stood. Amy quickly bent down to whisper to Ruth.

"You don't have to do this yet," she whispered. "This is a ritual we do to recognize our relationship with God and his son Jesus. We'll be right back."

Amy followed Paul forward and took communion, and they returned to their seats.

After the benediction, they filed out of the hall, and Amy looked at Ruth.

"That must have seemed very strange to you," she said.

"I read some of these things in the Holy Bible. I did not understand it then. I think I see now. You must take the essence of Jesus in." Ruth moved her hands toward her mouth and then to her heart. "Jesus becomes part of you."

"That's about right," Amy said.

"It is a ritual we do to remind us just what Jesus sacrificed, and that we need to take that sacrifice to heart," Paul joined in. "It also reminds us that as a result of that sacrifice, we have grace. Without grace, we have nothing."

TWENTY

A House

Amy trudged through the warm morning rain with Paul to the community hall. Yesterday's worship service had filled them with joy after so much that had happened in the last couple of weeks. Now, they were back to the usual activities, but with fewer perimeter watches and more work with patrons getting houses ready to become homes.

Today, they were heading back to the hall to find out what plans had been made or changed after the last few days.

"Paul, I've been thinking," Amy said.

"Now I'm worried," he replied, chuckling.

She punched his shoulder.

"Get serious, please. I'm thinking we should get married sooner than I said before."

Paul stopped and looked at her.

"Are you sure?"

"Well, we need a place to live first," she said wiping rain from her face. "That will take a little time to prepare. But soon after that, yes, we should."

"Oh," Paul said and started walking again. "Well, I've had my eye on this little place. I'll take you around to see it. It isn't far, and it's convenient to our parents' homes and to our patron friends."

"Okay, then let's do that as soon as we can." She caught up and slipped her arm through his. "Soon."

They finally ran up the steps to the hall and shook off the wet on the porch before going inside. Elder Franklin, Brad, James, Ron, Lucy, and George Linderman were there with Harold, Ruth, and a few other patrons.

"Good," the elder said, "we're all here now. Let's gather around the table so we can talk."

James took the head of the table as they sat and started handing out some sheets of paper. In his usual style, James had the topics of conversation organized into three general areas, with a lot of bullets in the fine print.

"We have to organize some of the work to more quickly finish things before the fall. If we have another bruising winter, like the last one, we'll need our permanent shelters and homes up to snuff. Flynn is going to work with teams to clean up houses, make repairs, and help fix some things on our common buildings that have been—deferred maintenance." James smiled, and Ron chuckled. "Lucy, you'll be working with him, since we can't seem to separate you two."

James paused until the laughter subsided.

"There are some human/patron projects there," he pointed to the second topic on his sheet. "Most involving examining the reactors, figuring out how they work, and finding ways to apply their power and capability to our homes and community.

"The third topic is a new mission."

Amy and Paul looked at each other. *Uh-oh*, Amy thought.

"Elder Franklin, Amy, and Paul will work on organizing a mission back to Washington, D.C. The government is struggling, according to our last communication. They made progress on getting buildings useable and finding places to live, but power and water services have finally failed. This mission depends, to a large degree, on the research into the patron technology. We want to take something to D.C. that will get them working again."

Amy looked at Harold and Ruth, and they nodded back. *Good*, she thought, *they're on board*.

"How are we going to communicate our plan to them?" Paul asked. "They'll need to be prepared for what we bring along. I can imagine their reaction to flying saucers showing up on the mall."

"We've been using ham radios," James said. "But with their power issues, that isn't very reliable. We're going to send a courier to relay important messages. The trip isn't as dangerous as it was before."

James looked at Paul.

"What I want you to do is work with Harold and his friends, and figure out how to make three more saucers and another of the transports," he said. James tensed for a moment, then shook himself and rubbed his right shoulder. "I'm going to work with our engineers and the patrons to make some reactors and some of the patron machines. That's what we're going to take to D.C. Along with a few patrons and a couple of our nuclear engineers. That'll be enough to get that city buzzing again."

James turned to Amy and Elder Franklin.

"You two, along with Ruth, will get a plan together of who is going, and prepare D.C. by crafting messages that will prepare them for the shock of seeing the saucers and what we're bringing. They do have some military units, and the last thing we want is to have them start shooting at us when we show up.

"Based on the other activities, you'll come up with a time for when we go to D.C."

Amy nodded and looked at the elder and Ruth. Ruth smiled.

"This is good work," Ruth said. "We will help all we can."

#

Amy worked at the stove. The sunny days had banked up the batteries so she was able to use it to make a hearty breakfast of toast and eggs—scrambled with onions, mushrooms, chopped spinach, and goat cheese.

Coffee was already on the table where Ruth and Elder Franklin sat, waiting for the main course.

"How much should we tell D.C. about the patrons in the first message?" she asked as she scooped out the scramble from the pan into a large bowl. "I don't know how paranoid they might be."

She carried the bowl to the table and served Ruth and the elder with a big spoon.

"This smells so good," Ruth said breathing deeply.

"You'll like it much more than those MREs," the elder said.

"Would you bless it, elder?" Amy sat at the table.

"Of course," he bowed his head. "Father, we ask that you bless this food to nourish our bodies for your service. We thank you for your generous blessings, for our friends the patrons, and for this bounty. We ask this in the blessed name of your son, Jesus Christ. Amen."

"Amen," Amy said and reached for her fork.

"Amen," Ruth said. She reached for her fork, smiling. "The blessing is such an interesting thing. You thank God for what you have, but you worked hard to grow and gather this," she indicated the steaming scramble on her plate. "And, you thank Him for us. Do you think God sent us to you?"

"He may have," the elder said. "In any case, you have been a blessing. As for the food, yes, we worked to gather and grow, but God made the universe and all it contains. It is through His grace and creation that we have this."

Ruth nodded and took a first bite of the scramble.

"Oh," she said, "this is wonderful, Amy!"

"I think it's the goat cheese that makes it so good," Amy said. "And the eggs. They are nice, large, and have these bright yellow yokes. It is amazing."

The table quieted for a few minutes as they ate.

The elder wiped his mouth with a napkin, then sipped his coffee.

"That was fantastic, Amy," he said. "Paul is going to be very blessed being your husband."

Amy felt the color rising in her cheeks, but smiled.

"To get back to your question," the elder went on, "we should give them some indication that we have new friends, and they have special gifts. Keep it positive, but don't give away much at first. They need to know we bring a solution to their power and other needs."

"That's good," Amy said. She pulled up a notepad and pencil and started writing. She stopped to think, and get a few more bites of her breakfast, then wrote some more. Then she reviewed what she wrote, scratched out a word here and replaced another there.

"How's this, elder?" She handed the pad to Elder Franklin.

He read it through nodding. "Good," he said and handed it to Ruth.

"Yes, this is good," Ruth said after she read it.

"Well," Amy said, "I figure they probably won't be as receptive of you showing up on their front doorstep as we were. We were in the last stages of losing a life or death fight and really needed some help. Harold was the one who prevented that meeting from becoming a big mess."

"I knew Harold would meet you with a calm mind and help keep you calm," Ruth said. "We needed you to know we are not here to conquer as our bad boss wanted."

Amy smiled. *This turned out so much better than I hoped*, she thought. She cleared the table and did the dishes with help from Ruth and Elder Franklin. Then they took the message to the hall to get it ready to go with the courier.

#

Paul led the way to the small house he'd told Amy would be a good place for them to live and start a family. *Well*, Amy thought, *small is a relative term.* It had three bedrooms, two baths, a nice size great room and kitchen, and a bonus room over the garage.

It's smaller than our parents' homes, she thought, *but way more room that we need right away.* There were some new people and patrons getting set up in houses nearby, so they would have neighbors. She looked through the home. It obviously had been sitting for some time, but she saw no evidence of rodents or other pests. A few cobwebs grew in corners, and lots of dust covered everything. It was solid, though, and no roof leaks. It just needed a good cleaning out.

"So, if you like it," Paul said, "we can ... "

Amy held up her hand.

"We need to clean it up first. Don't talk to me about changing this or changing that. From what I see, the cabinets are fine. The walls, doors, and closets are fine. There is a lot of work here." She wandered through the kitchen again. "But once we get it cleaned out, I think it might work. So, how do we get permission to live here?"

"Done. I have permission from the community for us to live here already."

Paul pulled a rumpled piece of paper from his hip pocket and held it up.

"You stinker!" Amy came over to him and put her arms around his waist. "When did this happen?"

"Oh, about last Christmas," Paul said. "I wanted to get dibs on this right away. Even if you turned me down, I was getting ready to move out of my folk's home."

"Even if I turned you down?" She punched his gut.

"Oof!"

"Was there ever any doubt in your mind that I would accept your proposal?"

"I did worry a bit," Paul said, sweeping Amy into his arms. She hugged him back.

"When can we start cleaning it up?"

"I have a couple of days work with the patrons to get some things going. After that, I can devote a few days to this."

"I'm also tied up, but I think in two days we can come in here and start working. I'll gather some cleaning stuff from my parent's house and have it ready."

They walked hand-in-hand back to their neighborhood. Amy told him about the message they sent with the courier.

"I hope it is enough to give them hope," she said, "without getting their paranoia up. We're planning to bring the concept of the patrons to them in small chunks so they get used to the idea that while our new friends are not from here, they are good, peaceful, and helpful."

"Good idea," Paul said. "We're getting things set up to have their machines make some new saucers. I've been talking to Harold about making some modifications to the saucer blasters and the sticks. When we had to fight them in Wyoming and Montana, we were able to use their own blaster sticks and saucer blasters to destroy saucers and patrons. We're working on a way that the sticks and the saucer weapons can't be used on themselves."

"Wow," Amy said, "that's a good idea, too!"

"Well, we're working on it," he said. "I don't know if it will work or not. Our first two prototypes just didn't fire at all. We'll get it, though."

"I'm sure you will," Amy said, giving his hand a gentle squeeze. "I'm just so optimistic about everything we're doing. We're about to open the door to a whole new world here. Assuming the folks in D.C. accept what we're doing."

"I think they will," Paul said. "We have a power system that will last indefinitely, it requires little in the way of maintenance, and its fuel is just waste material. Machines powered by these little reactors can produce amazing things with just a little programming and some material shoved into one end."

"What material are you using for the new saucers?"

"Most of it is coming down from orbit. They are cutting up the old starship and bringing down the pieces. We're using those to feed into the reactors and output the parts of the saucers."

"Why didn't they just land the starship?"

"It is very large, or was," Paul said. "Something that large, no matter what it is made of, would collapse from its own weight in our gravity, not to mention the stresses of moving through the atmosphere. In other words, had they tried to land the starship, they all would've died in the crash."

"Oh."

TWENTY-ONE

Courier

Amy picked up the return message from the courier when she got to the community hall. When she read the return message from the government in Washington, D.C., it wasn't the response she'd expected or hoped for.

"Greetings. Thank you for the communication. While we would welcome help in resolving our power and water service issues, we are not willing to abdicate our position or responsibility to some un-vetted 'friends' without due consideration. For all we know, your community has been subjugated by a rogue group, and this is an attempt to ensnare our government.

"We would like some specifics on who your 'friends' are and what technology they bring to the table. We also want to know what price they demand for this help. Sincerely, President Miranda Collins."

This is going to be tougher than I thought. Amy put her head in her hands and prayed. She prayed for the government, for the president, for the community. She asked God for a miracle—or guidance, if that was more appropriate. She'd been in this prayer warrior mode for an hour when Lucy came by and sat quietly nearby.

"Are you alive?"

Amy slowly pulled her hands away and looked at her friend.

"Yeah. I'm praying." Amy wiped her eyes and rubbed her face.

"So, what's going on?"

Amy pushed the message from D.C. across the table. Lucy read it and looked up at Amy.

"This isn't good," she said.

"No," Amy agreed. "I'm not sure if we can convince the person who wrote this—President Miranda Collins, if that's who wrote it—that we are all on the up and up. She's basically saying we are trying to scam them."

"I'm thinking a face-to-face meeting is the only way to resolve this."

"You're probably right," Amy said. "I need to talk to Elder Franklin and Ruth about this."

Amy stood prepared to leave to find Elder Franklin when he walked up to the table. She took her seat again, then passed the message to the elder. He sat and read the message.

"Oh, my," he said. "This is not good. I had hoped they would be at least a little cooperative." He turned as Ruth entered the hall and waved her over. "Let's let her read it."

Ruth joined them and read the message when Elder Franklin passed it to her. As she finished, her hand covered her mouth. Tears filled her large eyes.

"They are so distrustful," she said. "This may be difficult."

"Lucy suggested a face-to-face meeting," Amy said. "Maybe that would allow us to better communicate what's going on."

The elder nodded his gray head and massaged his face with his hands.

"I think you are correct. We need to set up a meeting in some neutral place so we can resolve this trust issue if nothing else."

"The location should be far enough out from D.C. to be neutral, but close enough that they can make it in a reasonable time," Amy said. "They are probably having the same problem with vehicles and fuel we had. We can get there early in the saucers, hide them, and watch as the D.C. folks arrive."

"Good thinking," the elder said. He went over to another table where James kept a map of the region. He traced with his finger along a route from Raleigh to D.C. and stopped. "Ruther Glenn. We'll offer to meet them at Ruther Glenn. It is right on Interstate 95, easy for them to get to, and—if memory serves—it is open enough that we can meet right on the road without worrying about an ambush."

"Sounds like a plan," Lucy said.

Amy started to craft a message back to President Collins. "How do you spell that place?"

Elder Franklin spelled it out for her from the map. "Say we will meet on the roadway about a mile north of the interchange at noon. That covers our concerns for an ambush and should allay any fears they may have. I know they have a military force, I just don't know how large, how well equipped, or how well supplied. We did take some of the weapons cache when we were there."

"I'm sure there were others we didn't find, or could have accessed," Amy said, remembering how Ron used explosives to blow the armory vaults open. "I think we were blessed with what we got."

Lucy watched as Amy finished up the message, made some changes to wording, then handed it to Elder Franklin. The elder read it then passed it to Ruth.

"Good," he said, then looked at a calendar. "Good. Make the date in ten days. That gives the courier time to get back with a confirmation and any changes they might want. And it gives them plenty of time to get to the site. Let's get this cleaned up and to the courier."

Amy got the note from Ruth and rewrote it on a fresh sheet with the date suggested. Nice and clean. She made the signature line 'Elder Raymond Franklin, the community.' When she passed the message back to the elder, he scanned through it, then signed at the bottom.

"Good," he said. "Let's hope this works, and we can get this trust issue resolved soon."

#

Amy scrubbed the cabinets and counters in the kitchen while Paul used a vacuum to clean the floors. *The house was starting to look better already*, she thought. They would still need to scrub the hard surface floors and bring in a carpet cleaner for the rest. Then, there were walls and ceilings, and the closets.

The previous occupants' clothing and belongings were still in the closets. When she got to that part, one of the patrons would bring one of their fusion reactor powered machines around and they would feed the contents of the closets and the cabinets into it.

In a way, it was like a waste disposal that could then turn around and make things they needed. Amy didn't pretend to understand the whole process or how it worked. She was just thankful the patrons had it and were sharing.

She hauled another box of canned and packaged food out to the end of the driveway in front of the house. All of it was unsafe, expired, or spoiled. Most of the cans bulged. Several boxes filled with similar items were stacked there, waiting for the machine. She wiped the sweat from her brow with the back of her gloved hand.

The late summer days were warm and humid. At least this day, there was no rain. She saw a few scattered clouds floating across the blue Carolina sky.

One of the next jobs she would tackle would be the refrigerator. She wasn't looking forward to that. It'd been closed up for more than two years, and she was certain whatever was in there would be gross and disgusting. Still, it had to be done.

If the refrigerator still worked, they would be able to safely store food in it once one of the little fusion reactor was installed in the house to provide constant, useable, reliable power. The human engineers and patrons had worked out a design for household reactors in a few days and were already producing and installing them.

Back in the house, Amy got a paper face mask from her bag of cleaning materials. As she'd done numerous times in Washington, D.C., she smeared mentholated cream on the inside of it. Then she covered her nose and mouth with the mask, pressed the clip at the top to keep it on her nose, and slipped the elastic bands around her ears.

Okay, 'fridge, she thought, *you're next.*

#

The courier was back, and Amy ran to the hall to see what the response was to the last message. *Oh, please, God, let this be positive,* she prayed.

Elder Franklin and Ruth both hurried to the hall and met Amy at the front door.

"He's inside," the elder said.

Amy sat at the table next to Ruth as the courier handed the message to the elder. He carefully opened the envelope and read. Then he passed the message to Amy and Ruth.

"Greetings: We accept your invitation to parlay on the date and time requested. However, we insist on meeting one mile south of the interchange at Ruther Glenn. We will bring three representatives, you will bring three representatives. Both sides will carry a white flag to the meeting point. No weapons.

"Sincerely, President Miranda Collins."

"Short and sweet," Amy said. "At least she's open to meeting."

"We have six days to prepare," Elder Franklin said. "Ruth, Amy, and myself will be the three going to the meeting. I'll have Brad bring a contingent from our security force, and they will hide the saucers—we'll bring two—and be prepared for treachery."

Amy nodded. "I wish this were a better example of how humans can cooperate," she said to Ruth. "I do not know what brought on this distrust from D.C."

"I suspect that they may misunderstand about our recent fight with the horde," the elder said. "Some of our last radio contacts with them were desperate, just before the patrons showed up. I think they just assume the worst."

"Well, we will either dazzle them with our brilliance when we parlay," Amy said, "or terrify them that aliens have landed. I think Ruth will shock them."

"Yes, probably," Ruth said. "But we can make it hard to see me until they are very close. I will be a surprise, but I hope we can make it a pleasant one."

"We might be able to do that," the elder said. "Maybe some regular human clothing and a hoodie. They might think you are a young person until they get up close."

"Worth a try," Amy said. She got the notepad and scribbled out a quick note. "Let's send this back."

The elder read her note, then let Ruth read it.

"That works. Just agree to their conditions and we'll get ready."

Amy wrote out the message on a fresh page, the elder signed it, and they gave it to the courier.

Later, Amy entered the house she and Paul would soon share. Two days of hard work showed. The carpets were dried after being cleaned, the floors shined from scrubbing, and the smell had dissipated from the spoiled food in the now clean, disinfected, and empty refrigerator. The patron with the machine had removed the boxes at the end of the driveway.

Now the closets needed cleaning out. She pulled a large box over to the first closet and started filling it.

TWENTY-TWO

Trust Issues

Elder Franklin helped Amy carry a long, folding table up the ramp of one of the saucers going to the meeting. Others were carrying folding chairs, and one was carrying the furled white flag. Dawn wouldn't break in the east for at least another hour.

Brad had picked out six of the human security force and six patrons, and they were boarding the saucers. A human pilot was on one saucer, and a patron on the other. This was going to be a fully integrated mission, he'd said.

Paul waited at the bottom of the ramp as Amy came back down for her gear.

"I'm going to miss you," he said wrapping his arms around her.

"We'll be back for dinner," she said.

"I know. I'll still miss you."

She put her arms around his neck and pulled him down so she could kiss him. She felt warm and safe in his embrace.

"See if you can clean out the garage while I'm gone," she said as she let him go and patted his chest. "See, you're already domesticated."

He smiled. "You might be surprised when you get back."

She shouldered her pack and started up the ramp.

"That would be nice," she said and waved. She watched him trot away.

Please God, let this parlay go well, Amy prayed. *I hope your plans for me include a long, peaceful life with him and some children.*

She turned and found a place to put her gear in the saucer, then moved up by the control console where Elder Franklin and Ruth stood next to Harold.

"We have Harold as our honored pilot today," Amy said as she approached.

"Yes," Harold said. "Thank you. We will be at the site in a less than one hour. I think that gives us time to hide the shuttles and set up your meeting place before daylight."

Elder Franklin nodded. "Yes, that is more than enough time. We may even have time to eat something before they begin to arrive. Assuming things go as planned."

"I bet they arrive early," Amy said.

"Yes, they will," the elder said. "Like us, they'll want to be in position beforehand. We have an advantage, I hope."

"We are ready," Harold said. He raised the ramp and prepared to take off. "I suggest everyone find a place to sit. This will be a fast trip."

#

Amy sat on the floor with Elder Franklin. Harold flew the saucer faster than she'd experienced before, and followed the main freeway toward Ruther Glenn. She could feel the turns and twists as Harold followed the road or changed elevation as the terrain rose and fell. She could see he was focused on the screen, which displayed a night-vision, negative image of the route ahead.

"These are incredible craft," the elder said. "I can see why we want to build a few more of them."

"Yeah," Amy agreed. "But, we need to add seating and not just the harnesses."

Elder Franklin chuckled at that. "The patrons will use a lot of the material from their starship, but that won't last forever. We'll have to find some places that they can mine for more materials at some point."

"I thought the reactors could make just about anything," Amy said.

"As I understand it, they need to be fed some specific materials to make the metal alloys they use in these and other equipment. Mostly metal ores and minerals." The elder looked around the inside of the saucer. "Their alloys are surprisingly light, too."

Amy nodded agreement. The blaster sticks were light and felt like they were made of plastic. That was why people thought they were toys when she and Paul were caught in Great Falls, Montana. But they were made of the same alloys used in the saucers and other machinery.

She and the elder chatted a while, then sat quietly. Amy was about to doze off when the saucer suddenly gained altitude, banked around to the left, and then banked back to the right. She gripped the harness hanging from the wall next to her and was about to jump up and go see what was on the screen.

"I bet that was Richmond," the elder said.

"Oh," Amy said. She settled back down as the saucer slowly returned to cruising altitude.

About twenty minutes later, Amy felt the saucer slowing. She got up and moved to the control panel. Harold was bringing the saucer down on the road just south of where they would set up.

"The other shuttle is landing in a covered location," Harold said. "We'll unload and then get to our hiding place."

He lowered the ramp when the saucer was resting on the road, and everyone helped carry out the table, chairs and the white flag. They carried everything to a clear area in the median just north of the freeway overpass of a railroad. They were about a mile south of the Ruther Glenn interchange.

Amy knew the saucers would be tucked into thick woods on either side of the old freeway just south of the overpass. She looked around their site, using a flashlight to illuminate the area. She didn't think Brad or James would find this location ideal. She looked at Ruth then at the glow in the east announcing the coming day.

"I guess we're ready," Amy said turning off the flashlight. Ruth's face reflected her concern. "It will be all right."

Ruth nodded. "Yes, I hope so."

Elder Franklin set two large thermal carafes on the table, some paper cups, coffee fixings and a bag of pastries. "Coffee is on."

"Oh, thank you," Amy said and immediately grabbed a cup and poured. "Ruth?"

"Yes, please," she said. Amy poured a cup and handed it to her. Ruth then added creamer and sugar.

Amy sat in one of the chairs next to Ruth, while Elder Franklin set up the white flag.

"The shuttles are in their hiding place," Ruth said, then pointed to the button on her collar. "I will keep the communicator turned on so Harold will hear everything we hear. If there is trouble, he can respond immediately."

"Thank you, Harold!" Amy said.

Ruth smiled. "He said you are welcome."

The elder sat on the other side of Ruth, and Amy sipped her coffee, munched on a pastry, and watched the morning sun rise above the trees to the east. Frogs croaked in a pond nearby, and birds began chirping as daylight increased. A cool breeze blew across them, causing Amy to pull up her collar. Then the day started to warm.

She stood, poured a second cup of coffee, and looked around now that the sun revealed the terrain. It was broad, open country dotted with trees and shrubs. She could see a distance down the north and south bound lanes of the freeway. The median, though, was heavily wooded to their north. *I don't like that.*

"It is about the best we could hope for," the elder said, watching Amy. "The representative from the capital will either be friendly and cooperative, or we will have to get tough and persuasive."

Something caught Amy's eye down the southbound lanes.

"I think we have company," she said, turning back to the table and pointing.

Elder Franklin picked up a pair of binoculars and looked in the direction Amy pointed. "Yes, there is a vehicle moving this direction."

#

"I knew they'd be early," Amy said setting down her coffee and pastry. "I bet they were hoping to get a jump on us."

She watched the vehicle come down the road. As it got closer, she could see it was a large sedan with little flags on the front fenders. An American flag on the vehicle's own right fender, and a flag of the President of the United States on the other.

In the trees behind the sedan, she saw movement. But, the light wasn't yet good enough to make out who or what that movement might be.

She moved to their side of the table and stood with Elder Franklin to her right and Ruth a little behind.

"They have someone in the woods," Amy said to Ruth and loud enough that Harold would hear through he communicator. "Can't make out who or what."

The sedan pulled into the median and stopped. Three doors opened, and a woman and two men got out. One of the men carried a white flag. The men's heads swiveled as they scanned the perimeter. One nodded, and the three approached the table.

"You're early," the woman said.

"So are you," Elder Franklin said. "I guess this means we can get this done sooner. I presume you are President Collins."

"Yes." She looked at the three on the other side of the table. "You must be Elder Franklin."

The elder nodded.

"So, who are these two?"

"This is Amy Grossman," the elder said and indicated Amy with his hand. "This is Ruth."

Ruth nodded in her hoodie but kept her head down.

"She's shy," the elder said. He looked at the two men. "And, these gentlemen are ...?"

"My aides," President Collins said. She waved at one of the chairs on her side. "May we sit?"

"Of course," the elder said. He took his seat and Amy and Ruth took theirs. "May I offer some coffee?"

"You have co ... " President Collins stopped short, then straightened up in her chair. "Yes, please."

The elder poured coffee and passed the sugar and creamers around.

"You're just a child," President Collins said to Amy after sipping her coffee. Amy could see she fought to contain her pleasure. "It doesn't look like Ruth is much more than one. What kind of community is this that you bring children to a negotiation table?"

"We were spared much of the devastation and were able to defend ourselves against raiders and bandits," the elder said. "But life has been a challenge. Amy is not a child, by any means. She's one of my trusted assistants."

Amy could see the distrust in the president's eyes as she took the measure of the three across the table. Her gaze fell on Ruth finally, and she seemed to try to see through the hoodie.

"The zombie problem has been resolved," Amy said. The president reluctantly pulled her gaze back to Amy. "We were nearly overrun, but were fortunate to find a solution and end the threat."

"No more zombies?" A smirk appeared on the president face. "I'm really having trouble believing that story. Where could zombies have come from?"

"Actually, Asheville. During The Troubles, Satan left something there that created a zombie horde. Army Reserve and National Guard units from the Smokey Mountains kept the horde contained until recently. They came to us when they were no longer able to hold them back."

The president's eyebrows rose, but her eyes betrayed her disbelief. She looked at Elder Franklin.

"So, by what miracle were we all saved?"

The elder shrugged and nodded to Ruth.

"Ruth," he said.

"You have got to be ..." President Collins began, but her jaw dropped. Ruth pulled her hoodie off her head and faced the president.

"We came to help," Ruth said.

The two men started to get up, but Elder Franklin held up his hands to indicate they should remain sitting.

"It would be best for all that you remain seated and relaxed," he said. "We have a lot of ground to cover, and your attention is required. Amy, will you start at the beginning?"

Amy nodded and looked directly at the president.

"It's a long story," she began. Amy told the story of The Troubles and how she, Paul, and Joe went on a mission to set things right. Then she continued with the mission to Washington, D.C., and the fight against hellhounds and a demon. She then described the news Flynn brought to the community.

"But, see, this is just our part. I'll let Ruth tell her part."

Ruth sat straight and relayed the story of the patrons and how they were entangled in the twisting of reality caused by Satan. She told of her starship's own revolt and how they came to help the community.

"We did not know why or how we ended up here," she said. "But we are here now, and here we will stay."

Amy saw that Elder Franklin kept an eye on the three across the table during the long tales. She thought it telling that none spoke or questioned their stories.

Elder Franklin cleared his throat.

"So, we have much to tell and much to share," he said in his deep, rich voice.

"Well," the president began, nodding her head. "I'm thinking you have much more to give."

The two men stood and drew handguns.

"I see that the 'unarmed' part didn't sink in," Amy said.

"You think I'm stupid?" President Collins spat. "All this fairy story you've been spouting. What a load of ..."

She stopped and shook her head, then stood.

"It doesn't matter much anyway. We're taking you for safekeeping, and we'll see about your community."

"I would put your arms away," Ruth said.

The president gave Ruth a surprised look. "I don't think so."

Green beams of light flashed across the median, and the two men dropped to the ground.

"They are just stunned," Ruth said. "We expected treachery, so we prepared for it."

The president glanced back at the trees.

"No, there is no help there, either." Ruth said. "Please, return to your seat and let's continue."

"What?" the president said as she resumed her seat.

"We didn't think you would be alone, either," Amy said. "While we were talking our people found and subdued yours."

"How?"

"We have some recent experience in these matters," Elder Franklin said. "Now, shall we continue?"

The president eyed the two men on the ground next to her.

"They'll have a headache after they come to in a couple of hours," Amy said. She had no idea how long the stun would last or what the aftereffects would be. She just took the line from an old movie.

"You were right about one thing, Madam President," Elder Franklin said. "We do have a lot to give. You see, the patrons—as we call them—brought some incredible technology and are willing to share it with us. We've already made improvements on some of it. Like not killing, just stunning with the blaster sticks. We need a better name for those, by the way."

The elder nodded to Ruth who whispered something.

Two flying saucers rose out of hiding behind them. The president's eyes were wide open and her mouth agape as the sleek, shining vehicles appeared before her.

TWENTY-THREE

A Home

"Here's the thing," Elder Franklin said. "We did as you asked and cleared out Washington, D.C. We left it to you intact with a lot of survivors to help with the rebuilding. In return, we just ask for some respect and understanding.

"If it came to a fight, we would decimate you. We don't want to do that. We want to rebuild what we can and get things working again."

The president sat and nodded agreement to what the elder said.

"One of the most important things the patrons brought is a small, self-contained, shielded fusion reactor that can be made, configured, and applied to just about anything," Amy said. "I'll be putting one in my house to provide reliable power. The saucers run on them. Other machines use them."

"Have Harold bring the gift," Elder Franklin said to Ruth.

She nodded, and one of the saucers landed nearby.

When the ramp dropped, one of the human troops carried a box down and over to the table.

"This is one of those reactors," Elder Franklin said. "It is our gift to you."

"How do we use it?"

"This young man will go with you to show you how to make it work," the elder said. "There will be more."

"We need food, too."

"Well, that will take more doing. We have a pretty robust gardening effort in the community, but we need to expand food production ourselves. We're working with the patrons to build machines to help. We hope to triple or more our production by next year. In the meantime, we're happy to share what we can."

Tears streamed down the president's face. She struggled for a moment, then got hold of herself. She wiped her eyes with her sleeve.

"Are you going to take over?"

"What?" Amy said.

"The government. Is this a coup?"

"Absolutely not," the elder said. "No way. You are the government. We just want to help."

"We are now part of you," Ruth said. "We want to be family."

Amy watched the president. Relief crossed her features.

"We've been so desperate for so long, I was certain this was going to end badly." She took a deep breath. "We would be happy to work with you and the patrons. I think I finally see hope and a fresh start for our country."

#

"We escorted the president and her group back to D.C.," Amy told Paul as they walked to their house. "It all turned out so well. I almost thought it would end in a fight, but it didn't."

"I'm glad it didn't. The last thing we need now is another enemy." Paul stepped up to the door and opened it.

"Right. The big thing now is to get food production to a point where it will support us."

Paul flipped the light switch.

Amy stopped and stared. There was furniture. A sofa. A chair. There was a dining table and chairs. A television.

She ran into the master bedroom. There was a bed and dressers. She came back to the kitchen. Paul stood there grinning.

"It's all ready," he said.

"Yeah?"

"So, when do you want to get married and move in?"

TWENTY-FOUR

Epilogue

AMY SAT BOLSTERED on the bed. Paul and his mom and dad sat on her right, and her mom and dad sat on her left. She gently held her newborn in her arms. She still had pain and discomfort, but it was fading. It also paled in comparison to the sheer joy she felt having this beautiful little girl in her arms, the love of her life next to her, and family all around.

The baby slept after her first feeding, and all Amy could do was look at her with occasional glances at Paul. This little bundle she held was so precious, so special. It wasn't like she was the first baby born since The Troubles, or in the community. But she was still special, especially to Amy and Paul.

This baby began the new generation for the Shannons and Grossmans, and brought new hope for the future. For Amy, this baby represented her personal victory over evil, saving her beloved Paul, and making her part of the world a good place to live.

From their first mission at the beginning of The Troubles, then the mission to Washington, D.C. and the fight against the horde of zombies, Amy and Paul stood side by side and kept their faith in God. She'd seen Paul filled with the Holy Spirit when he stood up to Satan and one of his demons. She knew she and Paul were covered by Jesus when they found the source of the horde and rooted it out.

Without their faith in God, they could not have completed their tasks, and Amy firmly believed that.

A quiet knock at the door brought her to the present. She looked at Paul.

"Ready for more visitors?" he asked.

She nodded.

Paul kissed her quickly, got up, and opened the door. Elder Franklin led James, Harold, and Ruth into the room.

"Have you named her yet?" Elder Franklin asked in a soft voice.

Paul looked at Amy. She smiled, so he went ahead.

"Yes, we have named her. Her name is Dawn."

"May I hold the child?" the elder asked.

"Sure," Amy said and carefully shifted the child in her arms so she could hold her up for the elder.

Elder Franklin held Dawn in his arms and looked at her for a moment. "Father in Heaven," he said, "bless this child with love, health, beauty, happiness, and a strong family. Keep her as one of your special children for all of her life. May she be a blessing to all who know her and especially to all who love her. We ask that you seal this precious child's heart to Jesus, with our love and faith to help guide her. We ask this in the name of your son, Jesus. Amen." He gently pressed his finger on her forehead.

"She's beautiful, Amy," the elder said when he looked up, tears of joy in his eyes.

"Yes, she is," Amy agreed. Paul stood to the side, and Amy could see him beaming with pride.

The elder looked at James. "Do you want to hold her?"

James nodded and carefully took Dawn. Amy noticed he was more confident since the new prosthetic. It looked and worked like a real right arm and hand, thanks to the technology and skills the aliens—the patrons—shared. They had turned into such a blessing.

As James' turn finished and he prepared to hand Dawn to Ruth, the little knit hat slipped and exposed Dawn's flaming red, curly hair.

"Oh, she's going to be a red head," James said with a big smile. "I don't envy you raising this one. She'll be full of fire!"

Ruth and Harold stood together looking down on Dawn, and Amy could hear a purring sound coming from them. After a moment, she saw their eyes close and they murmured a moment. Then they opened their eyes again.

"She is a beautiful child," Ruth said as she reverently handed Dawn back to Amy. "We hope for great things from this one."

Amy smiled. She noticed the slight bump on Ruth's abdomen. "Thank you, Ruth, Harold. James, Elder Franklin. You are all so special to us. I'm so grateful we can all be in this community and can raise Dawn among you."

"We have some news," Elder Franklin seemed to bounce on his feet. "Lucy and Ron had a boy this morning. We helped as best we could and acted as family for them. They are resting now."

Oh, Lucy! Amy shouted in her heart. *Lucy, sister of my heart, I feel your joy. I look forward to raising our children together.*

"Did they name him?" Paul asked.

"Yes," Elder Franklin said. "They named him David."

"I'm so happy for Lucy," Amy said.

"She said she sends her love," Ruth said. "She is very pleased with her boy child."

"Tell her I send my love back," Amy said. "And my heart is overflowing with joy."

Dawn shifted a little in Amy's arms and opened her eyes. Elder Franklin bent to look at her.

"Oh, Amy, a little boy is a wonderful gift," he said. "But, little girls bring a special magic into the world."

<<< The End >>>

This is the third book in the ***Spirit Missions*** series.

Look for ***Sudden Mission*** by Guy L. Pace.

Satan, once one of God's favorites, now His Adversary, grows impatient with the plan and begins to harvest souls. In a fell swoop, he throws reality out of whack and the world into chaos. God calls on Paul and his friends Amy and Joe to set things right. The young teens journey through a messed up world—with a little help from an angel—struggling against everything the Adversary can throw in their path to accomplish their Sudden Mission.

With their world and their parents' lives hanging in the balance–and the Adversary sending everything from zombies to killer aliens to stand in their way–Paul will discover if he has the strength and faith to set things right again and stop Satan's harvest.

Look for ***Nasty Leftovers*** by Guy L. Pace.

Reality is back on track, but the world is devastated with only a remnant of humanity left. On a mission to restore Washington, D.C., Paul Shannon and Amy Grossman must face a sinister presence left behind by Satan. In the ensuing battle, physical and spiritual warfare is waged against the possessed, hellhounds, and even the evil presence itself. In this fast-paced sequel to Sudden Mission, can Paul, Amy, and their army of faithful triumph against such impossible odds?

MORE GREAT READS

Freedom's Secret **by Amy McCoy Dees** (YA Historical Christian Fiction) Keegan O'Malley has long since escaped the Jamaican sugar plantation and found freedom in St. Augustine, Florida. He vows to find his brother and childhood friend, his journey leading him through secret tunnels, over rushing rivers, and inside smelly, pirate-filled taverns.

Wheelman **by Brian L. Tucker** (Young Adult) When foster teen Cy Vance discovers his dad–one of the FBI's Most Wanted–is alive and well in Mexico, he must decide how far he'll go to help his family, even if it costs him his life.

The Chronicle of the Three: Bloodline **by Tabitha Caplinger** (Christian Fantasy) When Zoe Andrews discovers she is part of an ancient bloodline, she also learns that not all shadows are harmless interceptions of light. But Zoe, the daughter of the three, isn't just another descendant–she's the key to humanity's salvation.

The Chronicle of the Three: Armor Bearer **by Tabitha Caplinger** (Christian Fantasy) Darkness creeps around every corner as demons gather in the small town of Torch Creek, Virginia. The Destroyer has arrived, and the Reaping is coming closer by the day. Zoe knows it's her duty as the Daughter of the Three to hold back the shadows, but she doesn't know how, and time is running out. Will they find the answers they're looking for before all of Hell is unleashed?

Tyrants and Traitors **by Joshua McHenry Miller** (Christian YA) "Find the traitor hiding within Israel," the seer warns Niklas, "or our nation will be enslaved and your hometown slaughtered." So, no pressure.